A Thief in the House
of Memory

Also by Tim Wynne-Jones

Stories
Lord of the Fries and Other Stories
The Book of Changes: Stories
Some of the Kinder Planets

Novels
The Boy in the Burning House
Stephen Fair
The Maestro

A THIEF IN THE HOUSE OF MEMORY

TIM WYNNE-JONES

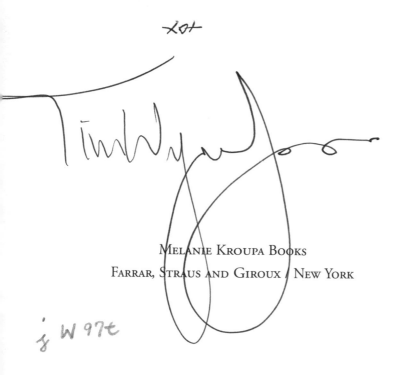

MELANIE KROUPA BOOKS

FARRAR, STRAUS AND GIROUX / NEW YORK

*The author wishes to acknowledge the assistance
of Maddy Wynne-Jones and Mira Goldberg-Poch, who read
the manuscript in earlier drafts, and Taya Ford, who was of
inestimable help in preparing the final draft.*

Copyright © 2004 by Tim Wynne-Jones
All rights reserved
First published in Canada by Groundwood Books /
Douglas & McIntyre Publishing Group
First American edition, 2005
Printed in the United States of America
Designed by Jay Colvin
1 3 5 7 9 10 8 6 4 2

www.fsgkidsbooks.com

Library of Congress Cataloging-in-Publication Data
Wynne-Jones, Tim.
A thief in the house of memory / by Tim Wynne-Jones.— 1st American ed.
      p.   cm.
The death of an apparent stranger in the Steeple family's old home
triggers troubling questions for sixteen-year-old Declan as he tries to
make sense of his fragmented dreams, random memories, and
unexplained coincidences, hoping to learn the truth about the mother
who suddenly left when he was ten.
   ISBN-13: 978-0-374-37478-5
   ISBN-10: 0-374-37478-3
   [1. Memory—Fiction.   2. Mothers—Fiction.   3. Family problems—
Fiction.   4. Canada—Fiction.]   I. Title.

PZ7.W993 Th 2005
[Fic]—dc22

2004053263

This book is for Xan,
who would rather play jungle than house

Une maison où je vais seul en appelant
Un nom que le silence et les murs me renvoient
Une étrange maison qui se tient dans ma voix
Et qu'habite le vent.

—Pierre Seghers, *Le domaine public*

(A house where I go alone calling
A name that silence and the walls give back to me
A strange house contained in my voice
Inhabited by the wind.)

CONTENTS

A Thief in the House
of Memory

PROLOGUE

Picture a boy's room. There is a bed shaped like an enormous red running shoe. The comforter is a golden map of the world. The curtains match the comforter but have faded. Time does that: fades things. The windows are deep, with cushions. A place to curl up with a comic book or a thought you need to think.

This boy is a builder. Models hang from invisible threads ready to dive-bomb his dreams. A Lego skyscraper sits on a low table. Action figures patrol a nearby shelf: Transformers in various states of transformation.

He is a dreamer. Above the bed is a framed picture of a house the boy drew when he was not even nine. A dream house. There is a book open on the bedside table. He might have just stepped out to get a glass of water.

Where is he? What's keeping him?

The curtains flutter. It's an April night. One window is open just a crack.

Listen. Someone is outside, someone walking too close to the shrubbery, checking a window latch, checking a door handle. There is silence again and then, suddenly, the splintering of wood. The sound is muffled—over in a second. Above the bed a Super Star Destroyer clicks against the Millennium Falcon.

Reach up and still the starships. Look at your fingers. They are black with dust. Run your finger over the jacket of the book. See the picture brighten under your touch? The boy hasn't slept in this room for four years.

There is no one at home. No one to hear a stranger break in, a thief with this whole, vast house to himself. Listen at the bedroom door. Open it. Quietly. The lights are out but there is a thin, wavering beam of light in the grand entrance hallway below.

Something has caught his interest. It is not easy to reach, by the sound of it. He seems to be struggling. He goes, returns. Now it sounds as if he is climbing. And then there is a rumbling sound, a furious shout, a thundering crash. A tremor runs through the old place. You can feel it buzzing in the bones of your feet.

Maybe this is how it all started—what stirred up the memory. For memories are like dust, in a way. They settle over time, almost invisible, but still there. Waiting.

SLEEPLESS IN CAMELOT

This is what appears to Declan Steeple out of the darkness of sleep: a river of molten glass. It seeps from the cracks and crevices of his imagination. Eerily glowing, gathering speed, the river surges toward a cliff top where it spills like rainbow-colored syrup, plunging to the sea below. Then, suddenly, it freezes in midair. It hangs there, shimmering before his mind's eye, like ice, but not ice, because ice doesn't have a pulse, does it?

Something is throbbing at the heart of all that glass. It starts to expand, inflate, as though an invisible glassblower— Dec himself—is filling that glittering mass with air, shaping it, making rooms inside it.

It is a glass house by an ocean glowing in the setting sun. But even as he admires his handiwork, he senses trouble— knows that such beauty cannot last. And he is right. In the space of a heartbeat, it explodes.

Dec awoke sweating, breathing hard. It was difficult work filling a house with air. He rubbed his eyes and propped himself up. Three a.m. He struggled out from under his duvet and sat, groggy and light-headed, on the edge of his bed.

What had happened?

There had been a noise. He looked toward the window. It was open a crack. Even though it was April and chilly, he loved to hear the peepers down in the swamp, the sound of spring coming.

He looked across the lawn. The lights were on in his father's workshop. His eyes strayed to the looming hill beyond the shop, to the woods made alive with wind, high up on the hill. There was just a fingernail of moon snagged in the skeletal branches of a maple.

He found his sketchbook and pencil case on the floor beside the bed and cleared a space on his desk. The dream image of the glass house had shattered, but the idea of it was still alive inside him. Could he draw it? He squinted at the dazzling emptiness of the page until his eyes hurt. Nothing. He tried to summon back the dream. The cliff was all he got. It was still there, solid, imperturbable. He had seen it before and now he remembered where.

There was a night-light on in the hallway. Noiselessly, he made his way to the stairs. With an act of will he carried the splintered remnants of the wonderful glass house through this most ordinary of houses.

Camelot: a split-level done up to look like a Tudor manor. An English country house plunked southwest of nowhere in the rough-and-tumble countryside of eastern Ontario.

Camelot. That was the name of the model in the *House & Garden* magazine, which was where Birdie found it. She had seen it there and pointed at it and said, "This one, honey." And so his father had built it for her. She wasn't going to live up on the hill, she said. She wasn't going to live in a drafty museum filled with memories that were not her own. She wanted a *House & Garden* Camelot. And Bernard Steeple wanted his Birdie to have her nest.

Dec made his way to the bookcase in the living room. He turned on a lamp and pulled out an issue of *National Geographic*. He knew most of them by heart. There had been an article about Highway One, the legendary coastal road that wound its way like a serpent along the whole length of California. Here it was. And here was the very cliff he was looking for, the one in his dream. He stared at the picture: the sweep of mountain, the swath of orange poppies, the dun-colored cliff, the pounding surf. Beautiful and empty. The perfect setting for a dream house.

The contest in *Architectural Record* magazine was for "students only." It didn't specify architecture students. It didn't specify an age. "The Shape of Things to Come." That was the title of the challenge.

His thoughts drifted. He laid aside the magazine and reached for another, 191, no. 6. Heiata was on the cover; the most beautiful woman in the world, with tropical flowers woven into her raven hair and a strand of black pearls around her neck. Someday he would build a house for Heiata. Being from Tahiti, she would want to live by the sea.

He yawned. Birdie would be getting him up for the school bus in less than three hours. Birdie—her morning voice like Chewbacca—at his bedroom door. "Hit the deck, Dec." The same tired joke, day in and day out. He hugged the open magazine to his chest and closed his eyes.

Then Sunny started to cry.

He heard footsteps and turned. It was the Wookie herself, Birdie, clumping down the stairs in her quilted nightgown, her arms wrapped around herself under her substantial bosom. She saw him and frowned.

"What is going on in this madhouse?" she said.

"I heard something," said Dec.

She looked at the volume in his lap. "You heard a magazine?"

"I got to thinking," he said.

She made a face as if thinking was something that should be confined to reasonable hours if indulged in at all.

"Don't go asking for the day off," she said, then ran her hands through her great mane of hair and headed into the kitchen.

He closed the book on his dreams. As if he'd ever missed a day of school. School was how you got out of here.

He turned off the light and followed Birdie into the kitchen. She was standing in the dark, outlined by the light from the hall. Her head drooped as she leaned against the counter. In the lighted window of the microwave, a Minnie Mouse cup went around and around.

"Ear bothering her again?" asked Dec.

She nodded. "Lemon and honey for Little Miss Sunshine," she said.

The timer dinged.

Dec looked out the window. "Dad left the lights on."

Birdie shook her head, yawning as she stirred a pouch of cold remedy into the heated water. "He's still out there," she said.

Dec remembered thinking that a noise had woken him. He looked again toward the shop, wondering if something had happened to his father. Then he saw him walk past a window. He was all right. Of course. Nothing much ever happened to his father.

"Had to get the war started," said Birdie.

"What war is it this time?"

She held up two fingers.

"The Second World War?"

She nodded.

"All of it?"

Birdie glanced at him wearily. "Just D-Day." She tasted Sunny's drink. Too hot. She poured some into the sink and topped up Minnie with cold water.

"My ear hurts." It was Sunny's voice, all wobbly, drifting down from her room.

"As if D-Day weren't enough," said Birdie. She joined Dec at the window. "It's three in the morning and your father is out there in his shop happily building some beach in Normandy. Go figure."

She sounded kind of proud, as if only a special kind of guy stayed up late playing with model armies.

"D-Day," said Dec. "That's a long way from the Greeks taking out the Persians at Marathon."

"I thought you'd be pleased," she said.

"Why?"

"Your old man finally joins the twentieth century. You're always grousing about him being stuck in the past."

Dec was just about to remind her it was now the twenty-*first* century when Sunny called out again. "Mommy?"

"Coming," said Birdie.

And Dec bit his lip the way he always did when he heard his sister call Birdie Mommy. Even after so long.

Alone in the dark of the kitchen he looked toward his father's workshop.

"Bernard Steeple arrives in the twentieth century," he murmured. "Alert the press."

Just then, as if his father had heard him, the lights in the shed went off. And in the new darkness Dec thought he saw, far up on the very top of the hill, another light. He stared. Must have been a shard of moonlight shining on a window in the big house. Where they used to live when his real mother was still around.

THE BIG HOUSE

"Wake up, gearbox, you're home."

The voice cut through the music in Dec's head. A horse-faced boy brayed at him, reeking of Hot Rods and vinegar chips.

Dec stood as if in a trance at the foot of his driveway as the school bus rumbled away. Half-Handed Cloud was in his earphones. Something Ezra Harlow had downloaded for his immediate attention.

Camelot looked even drearier than it had that morning. Fake half-timbering and fake shutters and fake diamond-paned windows. Birdie had been working up the soil in the garden, but it was too early for planting. There was only a garden gnome to greet him, and from the sneer on his face Dec could imagine what he was thinking. "Welcome home, gearbox."

Sunny was standing in the bay window, all five years, nine months of her. She was still in her nightie, having fussed all night. There was a cardboard box in her arms. Behind the sheer curtains her face looked ghostly in its corona

11

of red hair. Their mother's hair. Dec pushed his own hair out of his eyes, just a mangy shade of his mother's glory.

"It's time for my Polly Pockets to go to the Big House," she said, greeting him at the door. He could barely hear her over the music blaring out of his MP3: "Can't Even Breathe on My Own Two Feet." She held up the box. He looked at the assorted pastel-colored toys: Fifi, Midge, Suki . . . all the tiny gals of Pollyville.

"I thought you were sick," he said.

"Daddy says I need Air."

Dec shrugged off his backpack and crouched down to Sunny's level. "So why doesn't Daddy take you?" he said too loudly, pitching his voice above the clamor in his ears.

She stared at his headphones. "What are you Listening to?" she shouted, leaning close to his face. Clearing away her uncombed hair, he placed the earphones on her head. She jerked away and made a face. "Ezra-music," she said.

He switched it off.

"Daddy says he's had Enough of me for One Day. He couldn't do Nothing More."

"Anything."

"Not even Anything," she said.

"I can imagine," muttered Dec. "D-Day will seem like a holiday."

"Pardon?"

"Can't you wait for Birdie to get home?"

"It's Friday."

Which meant that Birdie wouldn't be home until ten.

Dec sighed. Sunny was a force of nature. There was no way out.

"Just let me get something to eat," he said wearily. Her face lit up. "Go put on some clothes," he added.

"I'm going to put the Polly Pockets on the pink dresser. They can keep Princess Jasmine company."

"Lucky Princess Jasmine," he said as his sister galloped up the stairs to her room. Her interest in the old family home was new. She had been a baby when they left, so she had no memories of it—good or bad. For Sunny it was a giant fun house. The fun had long since drained out of the place for Dec.

He heated up a slice of pizza in the microwave and found himself growing edgy at the prospect of going up there. He wasn't sure why. When they first moved, he went up all the time. Then the emptiness had got to him. Emptiness? That was rich. Steeple Hall was a monstrous time capsule, a house so big you didn't need to throw anything away, just close the door on one room's worth of memories and start in on another. It was his father's monument to the Steeple clan. There was over a hundred years of history up there, but the place still felt empty to Dec. It was like the shed snakeskin you found sometimes in the woodpile, beautiful but translucent and lifeless.

The timer dinged for his pizza and there was Sunny. She wore a bright yellow slicker over her nightie, yellow gumboots, and an impatient frown.

So they set off, Sunny chattering away like a spring-high

13

stream about Midge's flower shop and Suki's teahouse. Dec swallowed a bite of pizza and wiped his mouth with the back of his hand.

"Are you sure you're ready to part with those Polly doodles?" he asked.

"Polly *Pockets*. And I'm not Parting with them. They're just going to live at the Big House from Now On." She talked like that, in capitals.

They slogged through the gumbo of a low stretch of road. The big house was a game to her. Their father encouraged it. On her last birthday he had said to her, "The past is what happens when the present has no future in it anymore." She had hugged the doll she was holding fiercely, as if he was going to snatch it from her.

"Hurry, Deckly Speckly."

The hill grew steep. From County Road 10 you wouldn't know there was a driveway there at all, the grass was so thick. More a cow path than a grand entrance. Bernard didn't like the way to the big house to be well defined. No need to go advertising its whereabouts.

The driveway curved again and Camelot was lost to view. The old macadam showed through up here. It was easier to walk now, but Sunny panted a bit. She looked a little feverish, clutching her cardboard box to her chest. Dec offered to carry it. She turned away.

"We're Talking," said Sunny. "I'm telling Suki what a Great Time she'll have being a Memory."

One more year, thought Dec. I'll be out of here and this

whole place will become a memory. But when through the maples he finally caught sight of the tower, the peaked roofline, the many gables and chimneystacks, he felt an ache inside.

They rounded the final curve and the big house sprang fully into view. Light glinted off the glass of the conservatory. The newly budding maples shhhhhed in the breeze. There was always wind up here.

Steeple Hall. The words were carved in stone above the entranceway with a shamrock on either side. Sunny broke into a run. Her yellow boots made a galumphing noise on the wide stone pathway.

She waited for him by the door, wiggling like a puppy back from a walk. Dec dug out the long brass key. The tumblers turned. Sunny pushed open the door.

He smelled it before he saw it, a disturbing scent on the dry, old air. The frosted-glass vestibule door was slightly ajar. Sunny slithered out of her boots, pushed open the door, and stopped dead.

"Uh-oh," she said.

A glass-paneled bookcase had fallen. The spacious front hallway was lined on the eastern wall with bookcases, ten feet tall and three feet wide. One of those cases lay before them. Books were strewn everywhere. A bronze bust of Plato lay at Sunny's feet. She stepped back into her brother's arms.

Then they saw the hand.

Their eyes found it at the same moment. It was sticking out from under the massive pile of debris, the fingers curled into a claw. Sunny muttered Dec's name quietly—like a prayer.

He held his sister close. His eyes darted to the parlor on his left, the drawing room on his right, and down the long passageway to the study. No sound came to him but the steady tock of the grandfather clock and Sunny breathing fast through her mouth. Nothing moved. And when he dared to look again, the hand had not moved either. It was clutching something. He saw a glint of gold.

Sunny dropped her box of Polly Pockets and Dec was jolted out of his stupor. He lifted his sister up and sat her on the old church pew in the vestibule with her box of toys on her lap. She didn't argue until he turned to head back into the house.

"Just stay put," he said.

The bookcase was solid oak. It took all of his strength to budge it. Books still trapped behind a lattice of wood and broken glass tumbled out. His great-grandfather's legal books. One of them, as heavy as an anvil, fell on his foot. He cut himself on a shard of glass and pressed his hand hard against his pant leg.

The man was buried in law books, drowning in a green-and-gold sea. Dec knelt down and pulled away the rubble until he uncovered the man's face. He had never seen a corpse before, but there was a dullness to the battered face that quickly made him abandon any idea of heroic rescue. You could not attempt mouth-to-mouth resuscitation on lips that blue and swollen.

Then he saw the Chinese letters tattooed on the man's neck and gasped.

"Mr. Play-Doh."

He swung around. Sunny was in the doorway again, wide-eyed, clutching one of her dolls and crouching by the bust lying on its side by the door. "Mr. Play-Doh is hurt," she said.

"He'll be okay," said Dec, turning her away and closing the door on the grisly scene. They hurried down the steps and across the drive. Dec turned, half afraid that a dead man might be following them, but what he saw, or thought he saw, stopped him in his tracks.

His mother.

She was standing at an upstairs window, dressed as Wonder Woman, her fingertips resting on the glass, an expectant look on her face. For a few seconds the sun glinted off her golden tiara. Then she vanished.

"What are you looking at?" asked Sunny, looking at the same window, her hand shielding her eyes.

"Nothing," he answered, taking Sunny's hand.

"Not so tight," she said as they set off toward Camelot. "Not so fast."

Neither of them spoke again until they were almost home.

"Who was that man?" she asked at last.

"Nobody we know," he said.

But that was only half true.

THE WATER HAULAGE MAN

It had been three weeks ago. He was not supposed to hitch-hike. It had been drummed into Dec since he was a kid. But he was almost sixteen; he wasn't a kid anymore. Besides, it was an emergency. He had to get home, and when you lived half an hour out of town in deep country, there weren't that many options.

He hadn't known about the art club meeting to talk about next fall's trip to New York. He hadn't known about Dad going to Kingston for the day, either. He only found out when he phoned home for a lift. That was when he learned that Sunny's babysitter had a chiropractor's appointment and could only stay until five. Birdie wouldn't be finished with work until six.

It was that simple.

He had already walked to the western edge of town when the water haulage truck pulled over. Dec almost choked as he opened the door. The cab was so filled with smoke it might have been on fire. He started coughing and backed down the step.

"Jesus on life support!" said the driver. "Sorry, man." He rolled down his window and flicked his cigarette outside. He started making a noise like a fire alarm as he waved his arms at the fug in the cab. "Damn stupid habit, eh?" he said, and laughed.

Through the clearing smoke, Dec noticed the man's teeth. They were movie-star teeth, a little yellow but straight and lots of them. He was somewhere in his thirties with a terrible mullet and big sideburns and Chinese letters tattooed the length of his neck. But his smile was infectious. If Dec had second thoughts about accepting a ride in a moving smokehouse, the smile charmed him into the cab. He slammed the door and the water haulage man worked through the gears to get his rig back on the road. There wasn't much traffic on Country Road 10. There never was.

"Here," said the driver, reaching into his shirt pocket. He handed Dec a crumpled pack of Players.

"I don't smoke," said Dec.

"Me neither," said the driver, talking loudly over the drone of the engine. "Do me a favor and get rid of 'em." He burst out laughing again. "Save me from myself, buddy. Save me!"

Dec reluctantly took the package. He felt like the butt of a joke he didn't get. The driver's eyes were glittering or maybe just watering from the rush of air coming in through his wide-open window. Now he flashed his movie-star teeth again. "If I tossed 'em out the cab, I might get pulled over

19

for littering, right? And I don't want to give the cops no excuse. No way. Not with my rep."

Dec nodded. He slipped the mostly empty cigarette package into his breast pocket. For some reason, the driver roared with laughter again. Dec grasped the door handle.

"I'm already breakin' the law," the man said. Without taking his eyes off the road, he leaned toward Dec. "And you're my accomplice." They were rolling along by now. There was no chance of escape. Dec glanced at the driver, who was smiling through squinty eyes. "You're in over your head, kiddo," he added. "You're in *big*-time."

Dec stared at the tattoo on his neck. The man turned and flashed another smile. "You're thinking, 'Jesus H. Christ, I just hitched myself the ride from Hell.' Am I right or am I right?"

Dec shrugged, and that set the driver chuckling again. "You want to know my crime?" he asked. He didn't wait for a reply. "Course you do—being my accomplice and all. Well, I'm taking this here back road so as not to get weighed." He glanced at Dec. "I said *weighed*, boy. W-E-I-whatever. Get it?"

Dec didn't.

"You see, the Department of Transport up there on Highway 7 got their weigh station open today and I've got too much load on." He pointed with his thumb over his shoulder. "Just water," he said reassuringly.

Dec managed a grin. The guy was harmless. "You sure it's not bootleg liquor?" he asked.

The driver cocked an eyebrow. "Now, there's a plan," he said. "You got any?" Dec chuckled. "We could be a team," the man continued. "You source things out, ride shotgun, I lug the stuff."

Dec nodded. They were nearing Cupar. It was only fifteen minutes past Cupar to his place.

"We could start off small," said the driver. "Just water. We could steal all the water in Lanark County."

The laughter burst out of Dec before he could stop it.

"Eh?" said the driver enthusiastically. "You up for that?"

Dec nodded. "Count me in."

"Good stuff." The driver rolled up his window to block out the noise. Dec watched him reach for his cigarettes before remembering he had given them away. "After we drain the county dry, we could start in on milk. Dawn raids on all the dairy farms."

Dec laughed again. "Sort of work our way up to the hard stuff?"

"Now you're talking," said the driver. "You are just reading my mind, mister. But that's not the end of it. Hell no! I'm thinking the *big* money is in nuclear waste." Then he lowered his head and peered into his side-view mirror for a good long moment. He let out a showy sigh of relief. "Phewww! Thought we had the fuzz on our tail there for a minute."

Dec turned to look. The road was dead empty for as far back as he could see.

"I know this secret road up ahead," he said. It was a

foolish comment, just something to say. Just to keep the conversation rolling.

"That's good to know," said the driver. "Secret roads come in handy when you're messin' with stolen goods. What is it? An old prisoner-of-war camp or something like that?"

They were gearing down to pass through Cupar. Dec checked his watch. He would be home in plenty of time. This had worked out okay, he thought. Not only a ride, but a stand-up comic as well. "It's where the county road sort of swerves south," he said, slouching in his seat.

"I know the spot. A few miles up ahead, right?"

Dec nodded. "The old county road used to follow the river. But there's this big hill in the way and it gets too narrow for a two-lane. So they built the new road."

The driver nodded, genuinely interested, and Dec realized he had said too much. The deserted road cut across the back end of the Steeple estate. It wasn't public knowledge.

"It never hurts to have a hidey-hole or two," said the water haulage man, and he flashed Dec an easy grin.

Dec turned to look out his window. The Eden River came into view, turgid and brown, thick with runoff and yet still frozen in places along the banks. His companion was humming now. Everything was fine, Dec told himself, until the truck started to slow down.

At first he thought there was engine trouble. But there was no rattle, no smoke. The driver brought the rig to a stop without even pulling over.

"Is that the road?" he said.

They were at the very point where the two-lane highway started its long slow curve south, directly in front of the entrance to the old road. There was a deep ditch bridged by an overgrown and crumbling culvert. Beyond it the brush closed in.

You would never see it. Never. Not unless you were looking for it. If you were driving, you'd be too busy following the pavement, your gaze drifting southward. If you were a passenger, you'd likely be looking at the view to your right, where the Eden widened and was lined with willows, as pretty as a picture on a calendar.

"It's completely grown over," said Dec, backtracking nervously. "I wouldn't want to take a chance." He didn't turn to meet the driver's eye. He imagined this guy was crazy enough to try it.

But the water haulage man just laughed. And then he stopped laughing. He wasn't looking at the old road anymore. His eyes had wandered up to the tree-covered hilltop.

"Will you just look at that," he whispered.

Dec didn't need to look. Were it summer, the crest of the hill would have been a sea of green. In fall it was a sea of red. Only in winter or in early spring, like right now, before the leaves had unfurled, could you hope to catch a glimpse of Steeple Hall. Even then it took a keen eye to see it. You had to stare at the exact right place until the tower and chimneys and gables detached themselves from the camouflage of distance and forest and became something solid, something man-made.

Dec grunted. Then he made a point of looking at his watch. Once again the water haulage man put the truck in gear, but this time without a word. Another couple of minutes and the road curved west and soon enough they came to Camelot. A plain split-level you would never look at twice.

"This one is me," said Dec.

The driver applied his air brakes and brought the truck to a stop right at Dec's driveway. "Hey, now ain't *that* something!" he said. Dec followed his gaze to the mailbox on the other side of the road. It was a replica of Steeple Hall. His father had built it in his spare time. And since his father had nothing but spare time, it was intricately done, a marvel of craftsmanship. A passerby wasn't likely to know about the house upon which it was modeled. But when the driver turned to shake Dec's hand, the boy could see that he had made the connection, all right.

"Adios," he said. "Nice to meet you." He pumped Dec's hand. "Amigo," he added with a grin, his eyes shining like all get out.

OPEN AND SHUT

Dec Steeple slouched on a lawn chair wrapped in one of Birdie's shawls. He was pretending that the thin April sunshine was warmer than it really was. A book about the South Pacific lay open on his lap. It was a birthday present from Birdie. Somewhere in the middle of all this he had turned sixteen. "Isn't that one of the places you plan to travel to?" she had said. And the look in her eye seemed to suggest that she was ready to help him pack any time. But the glossy picture book lay unattended. He was reading the *Ladybank Expositor* instead.

The story of the intruder's death had made the front page of the weekly. Sunny sat on the deck happily killing off one of her Barbie dolls, burying her under a deluge of accessories.

"Read it Again," said Sunny.

Dec didn't have the energy to argue. " 'B and E Ends in Fatality,' " he read.

"Beundee?"

"Breaking and Entering. It's when you force your way into a place." He showed her the headline.

"More," she said.

And so Dec read more.

A local man died last Thursday night after a break-in of a deserted house on County Road 10, west of Cupar. Dennis Runyon, thirty-five, was found crushed to death under a heavy bookcase in Steeple Hall, once the residence of Senator Michael Shaughnessy Steeple, founder of Steeple Enterprises and Member of Parliament for Lanark and Renfrew, in the 1930s.

Runyon, who grew up in Ladybank, had not lived in the area for many years. He returned only last fall. He was currently an employee of Eden Mobile Wash and Water Haulage. Ted McHugh, manager of Eden, expressed his sorrow at the news. "He was a lot of fun to have around," said McHugh. "He'll be missed."

Bernard Steeple's son discovered the corpse of Dennis Runyon.

"Liar!" cried Sunny, her voice hot with indignation. "I discovered him."

"Well, they can't say that," said Dec. "You're too young."

Sunny made a face and then proceeded to squash Barbie under a red Ferrari.

"You don't want to call any case open and shut," said Constable Dwayne Hannah of the Ontario Provincial Police, "but at the moment it looks as if the death was accidental." Police believe that in trying to reach a valuable statuette, Runyon brought down the bookcase on himself. Constable Hannah went on to say that a forensic unit has been brought in from Toronto and the investigation would continue. There will be an inquest.

"But it isn't valuable," muttered Dec.

"What?"

"The statuette, Plato—it's not worth all that much."

"Because he's got no Brains," said Sunny, and laughed.

Right, thought Dec. The bust of Plato was heavy, hollow, and worthless. It made no sense. He read on.

Runyon had a record of petty thefts and misdemeanors dating back to his youth, but had "cleaned up his act" according to Clarence Mahood, a boyhood friend of the deceased.

The last resident of the Hall was Bernard Steeple, grandson of the senator. He and his family still live nearby. He keeps up the historic property.

He keeps up the historic property, thought Dec. His father: part historian, part janitor. He let the paper fall to his lap, closed his eyes. Began to drift into sleep.

Not a good move.

The nightmare is waiting for him, hiding just beyond his consciousness, a tanker trailer of a nightmare, barreling across the lawns of Steeple Hall, bearing down on the big house. Dec is at the wheel but nothing works: not the steering, not the brakes. He looks up and sees his mother standing directly in his path. She has her hands on her hips and a grim smile on her face—she isn't going to move for anyone. She is Wonder Woman, invincible.

"Deckly Speckly?"

Dec's eyes snapped open. Sunny was tugging on his pant leg.

"You were Sniveling," she said.

He sat up, wiped his eyes. "Was not," he said.

"Was too."

"I was thinking."

"Me, too," said Sunny. "I was thinking how the paper got it All Wrong. Mr. Play-Doh wasn't On the bookcase."

Dec looked at her, a little dim-witted. Sunny was staring at him impatiently.

" 'Member? 'Member you put your baseball cap on him?"

"What are you talking about?"

"Your Raptors cap," she said, patting the top of her head. "You put it on Mr. Play-Doh. You said, 'Yo, Play-Doh. Wazzup!' " She giggled. " 'Member?"

He did remember. The bust of Plato had been on the side table, near the vestibule door. His father had been painting the hall ceiling; there had been a tarp spread over the bookcase. When had that been? Tuesday or Wednesday. He had gone up with Sunny a day or two before the accident. "Daddy must have put it back on Thursday," he said.

But Sunny wasn't listening anymore. Making all kinds of concerned mommy noises, she began digging for Barbie.

Dec's gaze wandered up the hillside to see his father coming down from the old house. He had on his work clothes, his sleeves rolled up to the elbow, and he was carrying his red toolbox. There was a streak of paint on his arm. He seemed lost in thought, his chin on his chest, his hair falling across his brow—just like Gregory Peck in *To Kill a Mockingbird*. That's what Birdie liked to say. Bernard was her very own Atticus Finch. He was lanky like Peck and strong through the shoulders, but he didn't look so noble to Dec. There was a worried look in his eye. The forensic unit had been at Steeple Hall all week. They were finished now and Bernard had been putting things to right, making everything the way it was.

He didn't look too happy about it.

HIDE-AND-SEEK

Dec stood before a room with his name on the door: *Declan Shaughnessy Steeple, 1987–1999.* That was what was etched on the brass plate, as if he had died young.

He opened the door and scanned the room. It was decked out like something from a magazine. The bed shaped like a sneaker, his favorite baby blanket neatly folded on a pirate play chest, a Lego skyscraper on the low yellow table, a large Teddy sitting in a small wicker chair, wearing goggles and a scarf. It was Dec's young life laid out for some imagined audience of curiosity seekers. It had nothing to do with him anymore.

He walked into the room and shut the door behind him. There was a book beside his bed, *The Phantom Toll-booth.* He opened it and smiled at his homemade bookmark at chapter eleven, "Dischord and Dynne." He remembered liking the book, but for some reason he had never finished it. Maybe it was because they had left the house so quickly, as soon as Camelot was built. Fled from it like refugees.

There was an alcove as large as his real bedroom down

the hill. There were drawers built right into the wall and a walk-in closet, where every pair of sneakers he had ever owned sat on the floor in neat rows. On the rod hung every pair of pants, every jacket, every coat. He found the cat costume he had worn for his first Halloween and the Green Lantern costume he had worn for his last. They had both been superheroes, he and his mother. They had gone to town together that night—Wonder Woman and Green Lantern. "There's so much more candy in town," she had said.

He closed the closet and sat down at his desk. There was a lamp his grandfather had made for his father. It was shaped like a flying saucer. He clicked it on and light shone through mica portholes, greenish yellow. Alien light. He opened the drawer and stared at what lay there, a crumpled package of Players Plains. There was a bearded sailor on the front and three unfiltered cigarettes inside. Dec sniffed, made a face. He closed the package again. The top third of the cover was printed with stats about the number of deaths in a year from murder, alcohol, car accidents, suicide, and smoking. Smoking won hands down. There was nothing there about dying under a pile of law books.

They found Dennis Runyon's old panel truck hidden on the back road. "You feel guilty that you told him about the road," Ezra had said to Dec, taking on the role of shrink. Herr Doktor Sigmund Cling Wrap.

"I don't."

"Sure you do. But that's like a girl who gets her purse

snatched feeling guilty when the snatcher gets himself run over."

"It's not that . . . not exactly . . ."

There was something about Runyon Dec couldn't quite pin down.

"I have this snapshot of a dead man in my brain."

"We may have to operate," said Cling Wrap. "Fix you up with a few more megabytes of RAM while we're at it."

The image of the bruised and battered corpse had faded, lost some of its sting. But with this cigarette package in his hand, Dec could see beyond the dead man to the joker in the water haulage truck, to the expression on his face when he said goodbye. Dec remembered the tattoo, the movie-star teeth, and the terrible sideburns that looked like someone had pasted a couple of dead mice onto his cheeks. But mostly what he could see was the odd smile in Runyon's eyes.

A putting-two-and-two-together smile? The criminal sees the elaborate mailbox and recalls the mansion glimpsed at the top of the hill. Was that it? Was it an I-know-who-you-are smile? Because, of course, people in town *did* know about the Steeple mansion.

Dec had tried to explain to Ezra about how Runyon's expression haunted him. "His face lit up," he said. "He looked at me differently." "There was something behind his smile." "Suddenly there was this twinkle in his eye."

"Are we talking about Peter Pan?"

"That's my point," Dec had replied. "I can't find the words. Language is so lame."

But Ezra Harlow, among his many talents, was an intrepid discoverer of mysterious facts. "Take a look at this," he said a few days later, handing Dec a magazine article. "Researchers have found that the muscles of a face can create ten thousand facial configurations, of which three thousand are meaningful."

So the look Dennis Runyon had given him was one of those other seven thousand unmeaningful expressions. That narrowed it down. Now, when he thought about him, the grinning mug seemed to be saying, "I've got a secret, kid. Can you guess what it is?"

It was May but still chilly in the big house. Dec had avoided the place for so long. But you could cut the air with a knife back at Camelot. His father liked the quiet life and Denny Runyon had made short work of that. There had been reporters phoning at all hours for interviews—all of them denied. His father was as jittery as a jaybird. Birdie was just as bad. They wanted Dec to see a real shrink to help with the nightmares. As far as he was concerned, they were the ones who needed help.

But that wasn't the only reason he had come here. The place seemed alive again, somehow. Seeing her—seeing Lindy—however briefly, had brought her back.

He was about to put the cigarette package back in the drawer when a postcard caught his eye: The Fort Garry Hotel, Winnipeg. He picked it up, looked at the scrawl on the back. It was from his mother. There was another one under it. He had almost forgotten. And yet there had been a time when he read these two cards every day.

Dec. 7/97

Darling Declan, There isn't a minute goes by I don't think of you. I know I'm the world's worst mom. I have no idea what I'm doing or where I'm going but I do know I LOVE LOVE LOVE you to bits and pieces and don't YOU forget it. One day I'll be able to explain, but for now I'd better not make any promises I can't keep. I'm already up to my eyeballs in those!!! Help your dad look after our little sunshine. XOX Lindymom

The second postcard showed a panoramic view of Edmonton with the North Saskatchewan River snaking through it.

March 8/98

Darling Declan, It's been the longest winter of my life and the coldest. I found some work here. Temp work in an office. I play a bit at a little coffeehouse, sometimes. Your mommy the folksinger. My head's a bit cooler now. Maybe because it's just so damned cold. I hope you don't hate me. Hah! Bet you've forgotten your crazy mom by now, eh? Maybe it's all for the best. I'll try to write more soon. XOX Lindymom

Sunny was wheeling a baby carriage around the upstairs hall. "My Babies are Fussing," she announced. You could walk the whole way around the wide stairwell, which is what Sunny was doing, as if she were on her own private merry-go-round. She was pushing a full-sized regal-blue British pram containing seven or eight dolls. "I 'splained to them they Can't, Can't, Can't be on Television."

Little pitchers have big ears, thought Dec. "I'll be downstairs," he said. He didn't mind that she had tagged along. She could amuse herself for hours up here, and he had a feeling she needed the break as much as he did.

He made his way to the study at the end of the front hall. It was a gentleman's room paneled in walnut, a room of globes and framed antique maps, of masks from exotic places. It had been his grandfather's office and his grandfather's father's before him and so on back five generations. They had all been judges and magistrates, members of parliament or captains of industry.

All except Bernard. Bernard was a man of leisure, a putterer and handyman, an amateur historian and wager of tabletop wars. Whatever spark had ignited the Steeple clan had sputtered and gone out in Dec's father.

A mammoth mahogany desk dominated the room. On its expansive surface there was a brass lamp, an old black telephone, and a faded red leather blotter. Dec's laptop sat on the blotter looking particularly incongruous—an Apple iBook with a tangerine-colored plastic top. Dec had some writing to do: an essay on Frank Lloyd Wright for art history.

He made himself comfortable in the cracked leather chair, wheeled himself in close, and opened the laptop. He flexed his fingers like a pianist. He had found a quotation he liked.

"Architecture is frozen music," he wrote, paraphrasing some German philosopher. But that was as far as he got.

"Pssst."

It was like air escaping from a pierced tire. Dec sat back in his chair, surprised but not frightened.

"Pssst!"

How old had he been? Three or four. He wheeled himself back a step or two and stared at the shadowy darkness of the recess under the desk. She was curled up there. Lindy. She held a finger to her lips.

"*Shhhhh*," she whispered.

She had a rascally grin on her face. She motioned for him to join her, as if some urgent business was afoot. His four-year-old self obeyed, scampering under the desk and into her waiting arms. She pressed her finger to his lips. He could smell the nicotine.

"Why are we hiding?" he whispered, cuddling in close.

"Daddy," she whispered back, kissing him on the forehead.

Daddy? "Why?"

"To make him pay," she said, holding back a giggling fit.

But before she could explain, he heard Daddy's voice calling for them.

"Lindy, Declan, where are you?" He remembered how his mother pulled him closer, placed her hand gently over his mouth. And Dec could remember her body shaking with suppressed laughter.

Then his father came to the door of the study and walked in. "Are you two in here?" he asked.

Silence.

"Aw, come on now, guys," he said.

Silence.

"I swear, Lindy, I don't know who's the bigger kid."

He didn't sound angry, thought Dec. Just left out. He remembered waiting on pins and needles for his father to find them. But his father never did.

"Why did we hide from Daddy?" he asked when the door to the study had clicked shut. Lindy, sitting up cross-legged now, smoothed his hair back with her hands.

"It's good for him," she said.

"Good for him?"

"Yeah," she said, licking her finger and smoothing out Dec's eyebrows. "It's good for him to know how easy a person could get lost in this drafty old dump."

The whole episode came back to him as clear as a movie. He touched his eyebrows. They felt wet.

The door to the study clicked open. Dec caught his breath. He half wondered if it was his father, still looking after all these years.

"Deckly?"

He waited silently. Then Sunny was at the desk, bending down, her chubby hands on her knees, squinting at him sitting there cross-legged in the dark. She smiled with a rascally grin all her own.

"Who's It?" she asked.

I-LESS

Dec Steeple waited for Ezra, his lunch before him on the cafeteria table looking even more miserable than Dec himself. It was uneaten but not untouched. He had constructed an edifice of limp carrot sticks and celery stalks, a bagel and three olives. A monument to waiting.

He wore Roy Orbison dark glasses. They were almost ugly enough to be cool, but not if you were wearing a Green Eggs and Hamlet T-shirt that said:

I would not, could not kill the king,
I could not murder anything.

Dec was tired. He'd been up half the night again, staring from his window toward the big house, drawn to it and afraid of it at the same time. He had to talk to someone about what was happening to him. Where was Cling Wrap when you needed him?

He sat at the only table in the cafeteria with its own blackboard. Melody Fong and Martin McNair were using it to argue over an equation that proved the universe was a giant Twinkie. Arianna Osmanli was doing the *New York Times* crossword behind a veil of blue-black hair. Langston Parchment was silently destroying Richard Pergolesi at chess. And directly across the table from Dec, Vivien Ulman was busily writing in her journal. Dec became absorbed with the crown of her blond head. Hair, pale as a whisper.

"What are you writing?" he asked.

She looked up. "An ode. Well, a mock ode. Want to read a mock ode?"

"No, thanks," said Dec, staring at her jade eyebrow ring. It was the same color as her eyes. "Maybe some other time."

Vivien flashed a quick smile and returned to her writing. She looked particularly poetic today, in an Indian silk scarf and a faux leather jacket over a smocked dress that she might have worn when she was six. Underneath it she wore a black leotard and baggy gold corduroy pants. She glanced up and noticed Dec staring at her. "We call the ode 'Valley of the Dweebs.' "

"We?" he said. "I didn't know poetry was a team sport."

Vivien tapped herself on the chest with the end of her pencil. "Just me," she said. "But there's one letter of the alphabet we do not care to use today. So we are forced to say 'we.' "

Right, thought Dec. With Vivien there was always something interesting going on. "You're not using the letter I?"

She nodded.

"You're going I-less?" he said, just to be perfectly sure.

"Exactly," she said.

"You're going blind?" asked Richard.

"Not the organ, the letter," said Vivien. "A poet must learn to expand her vocabulary."

Martin McNair cleaned his glasses on his sweater. "To expand your vocabulary by reducing the number of letters you can utilize is a contradiction in terms."

"No, she has a point," said Melody, who never agreed with Martin on anything. "A handicap makes you find new ways of doing things, right? So Viv is going to have to find new ways of expressing herself—words that don't have an *I* in them. That's got to be good for a poet."

Meanwhile, Vivien had dug an old book out of her backpack, a novel with a torn cover. "We found a remarkable book at a secondhand store," she said. She opened it to the first page and handed the book to Dec. "Please," she said.

The crowd drew in close. He read the name on the cover, *Gadsby*, by Ernest Wright. He opened it to the first page and cleared his throat.

" 'Upon this basis I am going to show you how a bunch of bright young folks did find a champion; a man with boys and girls of his own; a man of so dominating and happy individuality—' "

"That's full of I's," interrupted Richard.

"But no E's," said Arianna without looking up from her crossword.

"Exactly," said Vivien triumphantly. She took the book

from Dec, turned to the front cover flap, and pointed at the part she wanted him to read.

"It's called a lipogram," he announced. " 'A composition which contains no instances of a particular letter of the alphabet.' "

The others looked interested. "That whole novel has no E's in it?"

"Not a one," said Vivien.

"Lipogram," said Arianna, writing it down on the margin of her newspaper. "Kind of like liposuction, except that you're sucking out a letter instead of subcutaneous fat."

Only Richard Pergolesi was still eating. He stopped.

"How long are you going to keep this up?" asked Melody. "I mean, you can't even say your own name!"

"Just today," said Vivien. "Tomorrow shall be an O-less day; the next day we shall go A-less, as we work our way up to the greatest challenge of all, E-lessness."

Nobody spoke for a moment. Everyone seemed to be trying to imagine an E-less day. No "the," no "he," no "she." But then, as if by unspoken agreement, everyone returned to what he or she was doing. Melody wrote something on the blackboard that Martin immediately erased. Arianna filled in a long word down. And Langston with a chortle took Richard's queen.

Dec rested his chin on the table. "How about U?" he said.

"What about me?"

"I mean the letter U. And how about 'sometimes Y'?"

"Been there, done that," said Vivien. "Yesterday and the day before."

Dec looked impressed. "I didn't even notice," he said.

Vivien leaned toward him, smiling sadly. "You don't observe a lot these days, Declan Steeple."

Dec didn't know what to say. Suddenly he felt as if all the vowels had been sucked right out of him.

Luckily at that moment, Ezra breezed through the door. The mighty doctor himself, all in black, as usual, with hair like a deserted crow's nest and tiny round spectacles that gave his narrow face a distinctly crowish look. The lenses were no larger than dimes and the frames were made of real tortoiseshell.

"Where were you?"

"Ah," said Ezra. "A good question but in need of some refinement. I assume my state of being is not in question, and therefore what you really want to know is what place have I most recently occupied and why for such an extended period."

With that Ezra sat down. Vivien moved along to give him some room.

"That was totally heavy," she said, and returned to her journal writing with great vigor.

"So?" said Dec.

"Urgent meeting with Marlborough."

Marlborough was the head of guidance. "What about?" asked Dec.

Ezra opened a bottle of water and glugged down half of

it. When he had finished, his eyes shone. "Dec, dear friends, one and all, an announcement. It's official. I'm out of here."

Vivien looked up excitedly. "You're expelled?"

"Great," said Martin. "I'll be tops in physics."

"In your dreams," said Melody.

"Is it because of that time you proved Mr. Merkley didn't exist?" asked Langston.

"Whoa!" said Ezra, holding up his hands. "I have not been expelled. I've simply been plarred."

Everyone turned to Arianna. She shook her head. "No such word," she said.

Ezra smiled like a cat on a sunny windowsill. "You know, I'm not going to miss old L.C.I., but I am truly, truly going to miss you guys."

"Hey. Help us out here," said Dec. "What happened?"

"Right," said Ezra. "The details."

"Thank you," said Dec.

"P.L.A.R. Prior Learning Assessment Recognition. It's when an institution takes into account the work you do beyond just your class credits. For instance, a summer job at the Chalk River Nuclear Power Station, making it to the Intel International Science and Engineering Fair, and, yes, proving that Mr. Merkley doesn't exist—that kind of thing."

"And?" said Dec.

"There's this scholarship to McGill that Marlborough figured I could try for, if I wanted. Now. He went to bat for me. Anyway, the long and short of it is, I don't have to do my senior year."

"You're kidding."

Ezra shook his head. "Montreal, here I come."

Vivien sighed and rested her hand on her heart. *"Alors,"* she said. *"Montréal, c'est très beau."*

"That's not all," said Ezra. "They've given me a job in the physics lab for the summer. I start July first."

Everyone cheered. Everyone except Dec.

"You're leaving in three months?" he said. It sounded like an accusation.

Ezra threw up his arms. "You can come and visit," he said. "You can be Igor, my trusty assistant. And when we've finished a hard day in the lab, we'll paint the town red."

Dec pounded the tabletop with his fist, just hard enough to collapse his edible monument. He looked up. Everyone was staring at him, Ezra the hardest of all.

"What?" Ezra asked. "I should have got your permission?"

Dec frowned, shoved a half-empty juice bottle into his lunch bag so hard the paper split. "It's just the red part," he said. "I mean, painting the town red. Where's that at? It's so trite."

Ezra pointed a finger at Dec and nodded. "You are so right," he said. "How about alizarin crimson?"

Dec managed a tight little smile. Red warning lights were flashing in his head. Ezra was leaving him. Why did people keep doing that?

THE WATER IS WIDE

Dec had been plarred: **P**assed, **L**eft, **A**bandoned, **R**obbed. Ezra chased him down after school and apologized. He hadn't talked about the scholarship to anyone, didn't want to jinx his chances. He said he meant it about Dec coming up to visit and if alizarin crimson didn't work they could try scarlet, vermilion—whatever!

"I'm totally happy for you," said Dec. "I'm just jealous, I guess."

"I'll only be three hours away," said Ezra.

"Three light years, you mean."

The school bus rumbled down County Road 10. A hacky sack flew past Dec's head. An elbow jostled him, grabbing for it. He pulled himself in tight to the window, leaned his head against the glass. He turned up the volume on his MP3: Crispy Ambulance. More Ezra music. Where did he find this stuff? And where would the music come from when he was gone?

The bus slowed down to let off another happy customer.

As it lumbered back onto the road, an impatient motorist pulled out to pass in a rust bucket with bumper stickers galore: "My other car is a Porsche." "I may be slow but I'm ahead of you." "So long, sucker!"

Right. Ezra was leaving Dec in the dust. His future was happening *now*. And Dec was stuck—here—in the middle of nowhere. Worse, he seemed to be slipping into the past.

He went straight up to the big house. Did not pass Go, did not collect Little Sister. The incident with his mother. It was a memory, that was all. He didn't need Herr Doktor Ezra to tell him that.

But it was so real. How to explain the scent of her, her heart beating against his back as she held him close? How to explain the way it filled him with a longing he couldn't understand?

He stood in his stocking feet in the cool of the front hall. There was no sound—no human sound. He shook his head. This was foolish. He had been hallucinating. He was having some kind of a breakdown.

The grandfather clock tocked; the house listened. His eyes wandered down to the floor. If Dennis Runyon had been erased from his memory, there was still an impression of him on the Oriental rug. Dec could see it if no one else could. He remembered how it had been rucked behind the corpse's feet as though he had tried to run and the carpet had tripped him up, an accomplice to his murder.

Of course it wasn't murder. Just an accident. That's what the cops said anyway. There had been the smashed remains of a little aluminum stepladder that Runyon must have found in the kitchen. The police had reconstructed the crime: the thief on the ladder standing on his tiptoes, reaching up for the bronze prize, slipping, instinctively grabbing the valance along the top of the bookcase, pulling the whole thing down on himself. The end.

But why?

There had been a sack of loot: silver and jewelry and china. What did he want with a clunky bronze statue? Did he really think it was from ancient Greece?

Plato looked down philosophically from his perch atop the killer bookcase. Mr. Play-Doh, as Sunny called him. His nose was missing but it always had been. The fall had not seriously damaged the philosopher. If it did fall. Sunny had seemed so sure that the statue had still been on the side table. And Dec wasn't sure it had been put back. He wasn't sure of much these days.

The bookcase had been restored perfectly, indistinguishable from its three stately cousins, each featuring its own bronze bust: Virgil, Descartes, and Shakespeare. There was a smell of fresh paint. You'd never know someone had died here.

Dec took a deep, shaky breath. He looked around, listened. Was that music he heard a long way off? He closed his eyes.

Yes. A guitar.

She was in the room with *Lindy* on the door. Her private room. She sat on a loveseat, her legs crossed, her head bent down close to the guitar, her hair hiding her face. She was singing a sad song. Dec stood in the doorway, silent as a secret, and listened. Smoke curled up in a thin wisp. She stopped playing and picked up a cigarette from the ashtray beside her on the loveseat. It was one of the fat cigarettes she rolled herself. He heard her slurping in the smoky air. It almost sounded as if she was sobbing. Then she played again, her voice like a soft wind.

The water is wide; I cannot cross o'er;
Neither have I the wings to fly.
Build me a boat that will carry two,
And both shall row, my love and I.

He wasn't sure why she stopped. Maybe he had moved without knowing it. Maybe she could hear him humming the song inside his head. She had sung it to him often enough as a lullaby. But he was six now; she didn't often sing him to sleep anymore.

He was glad she turned; he wanted her to know he was there. She pulled back the jumble of hair from her face, tipped her head, and smiled at him.

"What happened?" he asked solemnly.

"Nothing happened, honey."

"Really?" He so wanted to believe the noises he'd heard coming from the master bedroom had been nothing. "Nothing" usually wasn't so loud.

"Believe me," she said.

"You were yelling at Daddy."

She nodded slowly, her eyelids half closed. "I had my reasons," she said.

He wanted to go to her, but he could still hear her shouting in his mind and it frightened him. She seemed to guess his thoughts. "You need to understand something," she said. "When the big old wolf sinks his teeth in the lamb, it's the lamb that does all the bleating."

Bleeding? Was she hurt?

"You've got to watch out for the quiet ones," she said, not looking at him anymore.

He didn't like this talk. He rocked on his heels, his hand on the doorknob, not sure if he was coming or going.

With an effort she opened her eyes wide. She smiled. She rested her head on the gleaming curve of the guitar. "Come here, Skipper," she said, her voice tender and husky. She held out her arms and enfolded him in an embrace. She held him tightly, the guitar pressed against his rib cage. It hurt, but he didn't mind. Over her shoulder he could see her cigarette sitting in the ashtray he had made for her. He had dug clay out of the riverbank and then painted it blue with black musical notes. It sat on her school yearbook, a yearbook that was open to a page of photographs of people dancing.

Happy people. People having the time of their lives.

JUNO BEACH

Bernard Steeple was hunched over his workbench painting a miniature soldier. A hundred more were strewn around him, plastic, white, and lifeless. Dec waited for his father to notice him standing in the doorway. He looked up at last. Contact. Recognition.

"Hi, son."

Dec nodded a greeting and shrugged off his backpack. His father's attention returned to the tiny soldier in the tiny vise.

"Just touching up this squaddie here," he said. "Took a while to get the color right. K.D."

Dec walked closer. "You're painting him to look like Kraft Dinner?"

His father smiled. "Khaki drill," he said. The glasses magnified his brown eyes, made him look a little crazy.

Dec leaned on the worktable and imagined a wave of Kraft Dinner soldiers arriving on the shores of Normandy. He watched his father. He was giving the squaddie a face with the smallest paintbrush Dec had ever seen.

"Do you ever wonder what happened to Mom?" he said.

His father stopped painting for about as long as it would take to dot an eye. "What makes you ask?"

Dec shrugged. "I don't know. It's been almost six years. It just seems weird she never got in touch."

His father gently removed the soldier from the vise. "Is it all that surprising? Your mother never really cared about anyone but herself."

She cared about me, thought Dec. He reached for an unpainted soldier.

"Your fingers, Declan!"

Dec snapped back his hand.

"Sorry," said his father. "It's just that the oil on your skin will resist the paint." He was wearing see-through gloves like a doctor. Like this was surgery.

Self-consciously, Dec rubbed his fingers on his pant leg. It was only then that he noticed the wall. It startled him, as if it had snuck up behind him. It divided the workshop roughly in half. It was chipboard painted gray, the same dull gray that speckled his father's work clothes and that he had noticed on his father's skin from time to time lately.

"What's this all about?"

His father looked up and took off his glasses. "Take a gander."

There was an opening in the wall, a long, narrow slit a foot high and about four feet from the floor. Dec peered through it at a miniature beach right at eye level. It sloped down from grassy knolls to the sea, the sea stretched to the far wall of the shop. There were miniature machine-gun pillboxes and mortar emplacements in the knolls, sandbagged and camouflaged with netting. The same netting hung across the front of the window. Gently, Dec moved it aside. The far wall of the shop had been painted to resemble an early morning sky. Dawn was breaking on this empty diorama.

Bernard joined him, wiping his hands on a rag that smelled of turpentine. He leaned down to look, raked his eyes critically over the scene. "Juno Beach," he said. "The way the Wehrmacht saw it from their bunkers."

Dec stared in wonder. There were no soldiers yet. The beach was an obstacle course of tiny geometric barriers, painted to look like steel and concrete. There were rolls of barbed wire, and black poles sticking up everywhere.

"Rommel's Wall," said his father. "The black things are called Teller mines."

"Out of sight," said Dec. He had seen battlefields in this room before: Greek and Roman battlefields, Waterloo, and the Plains of Abraham, but never anything much bigger than a Ping-Pong table. This beach was close to twenty feet wide and twelve feet deep.

"Had to include a fair bit of ocean," said Bernard enthusiastically. "That's where a lot of the action takes place; landing craft, you know. LCTs and LCIs, half-tracks and ducks."

Dec whistled under his breath. "Ducks," he said. "Scary."

"Amphibious vehicles," said his father, not catching the

irony in Dec's voice. "I'm working at 1:72 scale. What you're seeing is less than a quarter mile of beach, the coast near Courseulles-sur-Mer. The code name for this particular landing spot was Love."

"Get out," said Dec. "That's perverted."

His father didn't seem to have thought about it. "It's just what it was called. Everything had a code name. Operation Overlord was what they called the invasion itself. Twenty thousand Canadian troops would land right here," he said, tapping the sand piled up outside the bunker window. "A very scary day."

"Twenty thousand?" said Dec.

"Just in this one small area. There was sixty-five miles of beach invaded that day. The Yanks thataway," he pointed to the left. "The Brits farther east. It boggles the mind."

He returned to his workbench. Dec leaned his chin on the sill, imagining what it must have been like to sit there waiting for the invasion. Love, he thought. How weird was that?

"It's strange," he said finally.

"Nobody's ever prepared to go into battle."

"No, I mean about Mom."

His father said nothing.

"I've been thinking about her lately. I'd forgotten how moody she used to get. Fun one minute, blue the next."

Still no response.

"Do you ever think about her?" He glanced back at his

54

father. Whatever pleasure he had seen in his eyes a moment earlier was gone.

"Not if I can help it," said his father, and leaned over a new white soldier. He was only a few feet away, but it was as if a gulf had opened up between them.

Dec shook his head and turned his attention to the beach. "We should go on a trip," he said.

"Excuse me?"

"Get away somewhere. You know, a holiday." He turned and leaned his back against the bunker wall.

His father regarded him oddly. "What's gotten into you?"

Dec shrugged.

"Did you hurt yourself?" his father asked.

"Huh?"

"You're rubbing your rib cage. Did you run into something?"

Dec dropped his hand to his side. "You could say." He peered through the narrow window again, scanning the painted horizon. He could almost feel the invasion coming.

"We never go anywhere," he said.

Again, silence. When he looked around, his father was gazing at him with a worried smile. "What's up, Declan?"

"It would just be good . . . you know, to go somewhere. Dad, you've got all the money in the world and you never travel farther than Ottawa or Kingston."

"That's not true," he said.

"Okay, Buffalo for a modelers' convention."

Bernard smiled. "When I was a boy, your grandparents and I traveled the whole country by train."

"No way."

"It's true. We flew out to Halifax and then chugged our way across the continent, from sea to shining sea. I've got a scrapbook to prove it."

Dec turned back to the beach and an idea occurred to him. "We could go here!" he said. His father looked bewildered. "Juno Beach," said Dec. "We could go see the real place. How about that?"

His father's eyes seemed to entertain the idea but only for a heartbeat. Dec watched the lights go out. "It's not there anymore," he said.

Dec threw up his hands. "Dad, it's France!"

"I realize that," said his father. "No need to raise your voice."

Dec shook his head in exasperation. "Think about it at least. We could run up the beach like in *Saving Private Ryan*. I bet there's a museum. You'd love it."

His father shook his head. "No," he said. "Right now, the only travel I'm interested in is time travel. I want to go back to Courseulles-sur-Mer on June 6, 1944."

He laid down his paintbrush carefully on its saucer of khaki-drill green. He got up from the worktable and returned to the bunker, where he leaned on the sill and stared out over the booby-trapped beach.

"That was the only trip outside the country my dad

ever took," he said. His eyes narrowed. "He came back with a knee full of shrapnel and what would be called post-traumatic stress disorder nowadays, but was called battle fatigue then; something you were just expected to get over. He came home with a keen desire to settle down, run the family business, and raise a family of his own. I was only eighteen when he and mother died. You know about the car crash. The thing is, I share more or less the same aspirations he did. It's as if I'm carrying on where he left off."

"Dad, I—"

"Don't understand," his father interrupted. "You think I'm an old stick-in-the-mud. Well, that's your prerogative, Declan. But I'd appreciate it if you would respect my right to live the life I want to lead."

He was angry—Dec could see it in his eyes, but you'd never have guessed it to hear his voice.

You've got to watch out for the quiet ones.

"Sorry," said Dec, but there wasn't much life in the apology.

"No, I'm sorry," said his father. He was leaning hard against the bunker wall, his fists gripping the edge so tightly that his knuckles were white. "I'm a little strung out. I guess we all are." He looked solemnly at Dec. "I do know this much, son. Going away won't help. You can't run away from your problems."

Dec's jaw dropped. "What are you talking about?"

"You know what I mean." His father's eyebrows bunched together gravely. Then he returned to his workstation, picked up his paintbrush, and started in on another soldier.

"Actually, I don't know what you mean."

His father glanced at him sharply. "Birdie and I really wish you'd reconsider about seeing a therapist."

This was too much. "I suggest we go on a family vacation and suddenly I'm nuts?"

"Clearly, you have been traumatized."

"Dad, I'm fine."

"So you say."

"It's under control. Stop worrying. You've got enough on your mind as it is."

His father regarded him carefully. "Meaning?"

"D-Day," said Dec.

His father frowned and looked down at the mass of squaddies still needing to be painted into life. "I wish this was all I had to fret about."

Dec made an attempt to cross the chasm. "Are you worried about the inquest?"

His father nodded. "I don't like all this attention."

"I know," said Dec. "But it might be kind of cool."

His father looked at him incredulously. "You think so?"

"Sure. I'm looking forward to it."

His father's frown deepened. "You don't really expect you're going to be attending it, do you?"

Dec was taken aback. "I found the body," he said. "I knew who the guy was. Of course I'm going."

"Forget it."

"What are you saying?"

"I've spoken to the coroner, Declan. He is in total agreement."

"But—"

"No buts, son. There is no reason for you to be put through such an experience. Besides which, you cannot afford to miss school right before final exams. This thing could drag on for days."

Dec folded his arms tightly across his chest to keep from punching the wall. "Dad, I could write my exams with my eyes shut."

His father was unmoved. "The coroner will send his constable out to the house to talk to you. That's all they need."

"But, Dad—"

"Enough! Do you understand? I don't want to hear another word." His voice was calm but his eyes, behind the magnifying lenses, were huge and blazing. There was a nerve throbbing in his jaw. "Now, if you'll excuse me, I have work to do."

Dec shook his head in disbelief. He turned, picked up his backpack, and headed for the door. "Work," he muttered scornfully.

"What's that?"

"Nothing."

"Declan."

Dec stopped and turned. His father folded his big hands before him on the bench. "I serve on the library board and

59

the museum board. I contribute time and money to a number of charities and I am a director of Steeple Enterprises. None of that is very impressive to you, I'm sure, but it is my way of doing my part and it keeps me busy enough. It is my choice. In time you will make your own choices. You'll go off gallivanting all over the world. You'll go to the best university there is, all expenses paid. You are a very lucky boy, Declan Steeple, and I'd thank you not to forget it."

Dec dropped his head and turned to leave. But his father was not finished.

"You came in here asking about your mother," he said. "This little display of yours—this acting out—reminds me of her. It's just the way she was when she didn't get her way."

Dec stared, not quite able to believe what he was hearing.

His father frowned. "I sincerely hope this is not a foretaste of things to come."

IF THE HOUSE FITS

Vivien wore a robin's-egg-blue burka to school.

"How do you know it's her?" asked Ezra. She was walking down the hall looking like a little blue pup tent. "She doesn't have any legs, any arms, any head."

Dec shrugged. "It's something in the way she moves," he said.

Ezra stared at him, then at Vivien, and then back at Dec. "Suddenly you've got X-ray vision?"

Dec smiled. "I wish."

She was at their usual table at lunch. There was a little rectangular screen where her eyes were. Dec could see them buzzing green.

"You look very springlike," he said.

"Thanks."

He paused with a french fry halfway to his mouth. Vivien was not eating. "Does that eyehole thing open up?" he asked. She shook her head. "Too bad. I could, you know, slip you a fry or something."

"I'm good," she said. "I can do without lunch for one day. I mean, all over the world people go without food."

Dec's fry suddenly tasted cold and mealy. "So is that what this is all about?" he asked. "A protest?"

"Not so much," she said. "I just wanted to see what it felt like. Experience it, you know?"

"And?"

"Well, it's pretty warm. But it's kind of nice in a way. Private, I mean. Like wearing your own little house."

"Oh. That's cool."

"Like a hermit crab. Once you outgrow your house, you just slide on out of it and find a new one."

Dec found himself thinking about a house you could abandon when it got too small. A disposable house. And that led him to consider how big a place could be and yet still be too small. His shoulders slumped.

Vivien leaned closer. "What are you thinking about?" she asked.

What could he say? That he felt like a hermit crab that had grown too big, too fast?

"There's this contest I want to enter," he said after a bit. "It's called 'The Shape of Things to Come.' You have to design a house of the future."

"Cool."

"Yeah, it's cool. Except my mind's been kind of occupied lately."

Vivien laughed. "That's perfect."

"Pardon me?"

"Well, I don't know. A person occupies a house, right? So if your *mind* is occupied, then at least you're on the right track." Her voice trailed off, as if the idea wasn't quite baked yet.

What surprised Dec was that he did almost understand what she was talking about. The mind as a house. He liked the idea. And then he thought how if his mind was a house, it was a haunted house these days.

When he looked at Vivien again, he got the idea that something was going on under the burka.

"You've got your journal in there," he said. "Is that allowed?"

Her eyes made contact with his, and even through the netting he could see that she was smiling.

"I never leave home without it," she said. She wrote for another moment and then paused again. "You know when you get an idea that you can't put into words?"

He nodded vaguely.

"Well, isn't it ironic that those are *exactly* the ideas you *have* to put into words?"

"Yeah," he said. "That is ironic."

She smiled and then her eyes dropped and he could tell by the movements under the burka that she was writing. The pale blue cloth bunched and stretched, bunched and stretched. Suddenly he found himself wondering what she was wearing under that thing.

She looked up and, as if she was reading his mind, she said, "About what you'd expect."

ON THE COURTHOUSE STEPS

Dec and Ezra sat on the curb across from the courthouse. The westering sun turned the sandstone facade blindingly white and glinted off the polished brass handles of the doors.

The boys wore matching looks of giddy admiration. They were staring at a muscle car parked at the foot of the courthouse steps. It was sprung high, with fat tires and magnesium hubcaps. A Plymouth Duster, something from the seventies as far as they could tell. There was a warning sticker on the bumper: "You toucha da car, I breaka yo face." There was a vanity license plate, too: "The Hood."

"They don't make 'em like that anymore," said Dec.

"Which is a good thing," said Ezra. "What would you call that color?"

"Crayon Sunset," Dec said. He was thinking about Sunny mushing crayons into her coloring book until it was stiff with wax.

Ezra leaned against his backpack and crossed his arms thoughtfully. "I think I'd call it Puke de Moutarde."

Dec nodded. "And such a nice contrast to Dad's car," he added, pointing at Bernard Steeple's brand-new Buick parked behind the yellow monstrosity. It was silver gray. No vanity plates. No bumper stickers.

"A Rendezvous," said Ezra. "How many does that make now?"

"Eight," said Dec. "The man could afford a Mustang, a BMW—a Hummer. But it's always a Buick."

"And he drives it three years then gets a new one?"

"Like clockwork."

"Awesome," said Ezra.

"Twisted," said Dec.

"But talk about product loyalty."

Dec leaned forward, his skinny elbows resting on his knees. His hair fell over his Roy Orbison shades, which gave nothing away.

"How goes the battle?" asked Ezra, his voice pitched just right: not too inquisitive, not too concerned.

"Which battle?" grumped Dec. "Operation Overlord is going fine. Dad's Waffen SS troops arrived yesterday, from some company in Texas, if you can believe it."

"Jus' waitin' on da beach called Luv," Ezra sang tunelessly, as he dug out a half-filled water bottle from his backpack. He took a swig and handed it to Dec.

Dec declined. He glanced at his watch. It was five o'clock on the third day of the inquest.

"What's going on in there?" he said. "I thought all they had to do was rule out foul play."

Ezra shrugged. "The circumstances are pretty bizarre."

"You can say that again." Dec picked up a small stone from the pavement and shook it nervously in his fist. "It was supposed to be open and shut," he said. "There must be some doubt."

"Did he fall or was he pushed?" said Ezra with movie-trailer drama in his voice.

"What if he *was* murdered?" said Dec.

"By who, Plato? Can't you just see the headlines in the *Expositor*: 'Philosopher found guilty of homicide twenty-four hundred years after his death!' " He chuckled, guzzled the remains of his water, and put the empty bottle back in his pack.

Dec didn't laugh. He took his small stone and started scratching the pavement between his feet, a ragged spiral in the hot asphalt. Then he noticed the small dark stain of blood on his jeans, from when he had cut himself trying to dig out Dennis Runyon. He stopped drawing.

"Maybe Plato did do it," he said.

Ezra stared at him, an eager grin on his face.

"I'm serious," said Dec.

"Well, if he did," said Ezra, "he must have really been using his head. Get it?" He paused. "The correct response, Dec, is 'Ha ha.' "

Dec nodded without looking up. "I get it. It's just that I can't help thinking about what Sunny said, about the bust being on the hall table. If it was there, then how did it end up on the floor? It was nowhere near the bookcase. Other stuff didn't fall over."

"I'll bite," said Ezra. "Why was it on the floor?"

Dec glanced sideways. "Tell me if this sounds too farfetched," he said. "Let's say somebody else is already in the house. He hears the back door get smashed in."

"He?"

"Let me finish. He tries to leave, but by the time he reaches the vestibule Runyon is already in the hall. So he waits—this other guy. He's scared. He doesn't know what to do. The vestibule door is open just a little. He sees Runyon. But he also sees the bust of Plato. It's just inside the door within easy reach. It's bronze, right? It's heavy, but not too heavy, if you're strong. And the neck is a perfect handle if your hand is big enough."

Ezra groaned dismissively.

"No," said Dec. "It's true. I tried it."

The grin faded a little. "Go on," he said.

"The guy in the vestibule feels trapped. What if the burglar decides to leave by the front door? What if he has a gun? He sees his chance. He steps through the open vestibule door—the carpet is thick, he makes no sound. He grabs Plato by the neck and whack! He clocks Runyon."

Ezra nodded very slowly. Then he pushed the tiny glasses higher on the bridge of his nose as if trying to get Dec in focus. "And the bookcase falls over out of sympathy?" he asks.

Dec turned back to his drawing, pressing hard on the etching stone. The line spiraled outward, a wobbly galaxy. "He rigs it to cover his tracks." He glanced up nervously and then down again. "You see, he didn't mean to hit the guy so hard. He panics. Makes it look like an accident. Because you can't say you acted out of self-defense when you crack someone over the back of the head, can you?"

Dec glanced over. Ezra was staring straight ahead, his tongue lodged firmly in his cheek. Then he took a deep breath and shuffled closer to Dec. He stretched his long arm around Dec's shoulders.

"Cut it out," said Dec, shrugging him off.

Ezra put his hands together in his lap. There was a difficult smile on his face, like the kind of smile you hold for someone fumbling to take a picture.

"What's this all about, Dec?"

"Okay, so it's crazy," said Dec. "It just helps to explain some stuff."

"What stuff?"

Dec threw his etching stone across the street. It skittered under the chassis of the fierce yellow car. "Things are totally nuts at home," he said. "My dad is acting so weird."

"A guy dies in his house. How's he supposed to act?"

"It's not that. He looks guilty somehow. This is my clockwork dad we're talking about. He's suddenly got this shifty look in his eye. And he and Birdie are hiding something from me—I'm not imagining it. There is something most seriously up."

Ezra didn't speak right away. Dec waited, not sure what he wanted to hear. It all sounded ridiculous now that it was outside his head. But at least it was some kind of explanation.

Ezra made a fist with his left hand and tapped Dec affectionately on the knee. "So you're saying that your dad might have accidentally killed Dennis Runyon?" he said. There was no sarcasm in his voice.

Dec folded his arms. "He was up that night, you know."

"I thought he was in his shop."

"He was, at three o'clock. But he could have been up at the house before that."

"Right," said Ezra. " 'Oh, darn. I left my tape measure at the big scary mansion on the hill. I guess I'll just head up there in the pitch-black to get it.' "

"He goes up there all the time."

"I know, I know. But you've got to admit this sounds like the plot of a B-movie."

"Okay," said Dec. "I hear you. I asked if it sounded far-fetched. Obviously it does, so forget it."

But he knew he couldn't forget it himself, no matter how unbelievable it seemed.

"If it was anyone but your dad," said Ezra. "I mean, he strikes me as more of a Mr. Rogers kind of guy."

"You've got to watch out for the quiet ones," Dec muttered. He wished he could tell Ezra about Lindy, what she'd said about his dad. But Ezra was looking at him way too sympathetically.

"I met Runyon, Ezra," he said, in one last futile attempt to get across his sense of unrest. "Runyon was cool. He may have been a thief but he was not dumb. I saw the list of the stuff they found in his bag; it was choice. What would he want with a stupid bust, which is worth a couple of hundred dollars, max?"

Ezra took off his glasses and rubbed his eyes with his thumb and forefinger.

"His truck was parked half a mile away," said Dec more urgently than he had meant to. "Why take a heavy piece of crap like that if he has to walk half a mile through the bush?"

Ezra put his glasses back on and stared candidly at Dec for a long moment. "Here's what I think," he said. "They really should have let you go to the inquest. Because you've got way too big an imagination to be left on your own with this."

Dec managed a small smile.

They punched fists together once, twice, three times. Then Ezra suddenly turned, craning his neck, distracted by something.

"Enemy plane at twelve o'clock," he said.

Dec followed his gaze to the courthouse. A hulk of a man had just stepped out of the doorway. He was in his thirties, as bald as a bowling ball, but with a razor-thin beard accentuating the line of his fat jaw.

He stood at the top of the stairs. He was wearing a

sports jacket, but he took it off and slowly rolled up his shirtsleeves.

"Get a load of the forearms," whispered Dec. "Popeye does Ladybank."

"Not Popeye," said Ezra. "Think of the plates: 'The Hood.' Any bets the Duster belongs to Clarence Mahood?"

"Runyon's boyhood friend," said Dec. "Nice work, Sherlock."

Mahood pulled a pack of cigarettes from his breast pocket. He looked steamed about something.

The courthouse doors opened again and Bernard Steeple stepped out, holding the door for Birdie. She was in spike heels, holding on tightly to Bernard's arm with one hand, shielding her eyes from the sun with the other. Bernard's face was grave. They headed diagonally down the steps toward the Rendezvous, but Mahood must have said something because they stopped and looked back his way. He was pointing his finger, pointing it at Bernard, and he was mad.

Bernard turned away and started down the steps again. But Birdie suddenly pulled her arm free and dashed back up the steps, her heels flapping. She went straight at the hulking man and pushed him hard in the chest. She was yelling, but Dec couldn't hear a word over the traffic. Patiently, Bernard collected Birdie, avoiding Mahood's eyes. Holding her around the waist, he led her away. She was flushed with anger. Her elaborate pile of coffee-colored hair had come undone. Bernard talked quietly to her, leading her toward the car. Mahood called after them, shaking his fist, until they were in the car.

"What was that all about?" murmured Ezra.

Dec stared at him, his eyes filled with foreboding. "I'm almost afraid to find out," he said.

SHUT OUT

But he wasn't about to find out anything.

"Clarence Mahood is a slug," said Birdie.

"You *know* him?"

She turned to Dec in the backseat of the Rendezvous, one pencil-thin painted-on eyebrow raised. "It's a small town, kiddo. I've known Clare since kindergarten."

Dec was suddenly struck by the implication of what Birdie had said. "So you knew Runyon, too!"

"Never said I didn't."

But that wasn't the point. She had never said she did! Dec was too flabbergasted to speak.

"It's no big deal," she said. "It has nothing to do with anything."

"If it's no big deal, why did you keep it a secret?"

"Pipe down. It was not a secret. Like I said, it's a small town."

Bernard cleared his throat. "To tell you the truth, Dec, we tried not to talk about the incident at all, for Sunny's sake, especially. And for you as well."

"Thanks a lot. But I'm not six, okay?"

His father sighed and shook his head. "Please, Dec," he said. "It has been a very long day. What is it you want to know?"

Dec made eye contact with his father in the rearview mirror. "I want to know what happened in there."

Bernard sighed again. "It's nothing, really. Just an endlessly detailed account of what everybody already knows."

"Mostly legal mumbo jumbo," said Birdie.

"And it'll be over soon," said Bernard. "Probably tomorrow."

Dec stared at the back of his father's head, unable to believe what they were doing to him—the two of them, together.

"It's been three days," he said. "How long can you talk about a guy falling over?"

His father glanced at him in the rearview mirror. "A man died, Declan. Show a little respect."

"A smart man," said Declan, "doing a really stupid thing."

Birdie laughed. "Smart. I like that."

"I just meant he wasn't dumb enough to waste his time stealing a piece of junk like the Plato bust."

Bernard held up his hand. "Excuse me, son, but that bust is not a piece of junk. To a common burglar it might easily have seemed more valuable than it was."

Dec stared out the window. "Common burglar," he muttered. "Runyon sure didn't seem common to me."

The comment was met with stony silence, but Dec turned to see a glance pass between Birdie and his father. Then Birdie turned again, a long-suffering look in her eyes. "As your dad said, it's been a real tiring day. How 'bout you just give it a rest, okay?"

Dec crossed his arms. "Sure," he said. "For now."

Again he met his father's reflected gaze. "When there's something to tell you, we'll tell you," he said. But his eyes said something else. His eyes said, What has come over you? His eyes said, Why all this acting out? His eyes said, I hope this is not a foretaste of things to come.

THE WILDCAT

On the fourth day, as Bernard Steeple had predicted, the inquest came to an end, with the coroner finding no cause to consider Runyon's death as suspicious. The case was closed without so much as a single line in the *Ladybank Expositor*. Things settled down at home. Camelot breathed again, but to Declan Steeple nothing seemed the same anymore.

The rains came. April showers a month late. Dec stopped looking for excuses to go to the big house. He just went. She wasn't always there. Sometimes he saw her outside the mansion but never far from it, as if she were a moon held in a tight orbit by its gravity.

She liked to surprise him. Shock the wits out of him. She would jump out and then disappear, giggling like a little girl.

One time they had a tea party in the dining room with real bone china and imaginary scones. He asked her why Daddy said scone so that it rhymed with gone and she said scone so that it rhymed with stone.

"We say lots of things different, your dad and me," she

said. "He likes to say, 'You'll never grow up, Lindy Polk.' And I like to say, 'Bernard Steeple, you're growed up enough for *both* of us.'"

Another time she wanted to bowl in the drawing room, using *Encyclopaedia Britannica*s for pins and a bowling ball she had dug up from who knew where.

Then there was the time they played catch in the conservatory.

"Bernard Steeple won't like this," she said, hurling the ball just over Dec's outstretched hands. It bounced against the glass wall, only a tennis ball, harmless. But when sixteen-year-old Dec watched the trajectory of the ball that his younger self could not catch, he saw the glass wobble in its dried up and crumbling putty.

He was two people in one these days. He was a child and a teenager, a participant and a watcher, a son and an intruder. He had thought the past was something that was over. Apparently he was wrong.

Late one afternoon, he ventured out back to where the sweeping driveway came to an end. The rain had let up for a bit and everything smelled alive. There were two garages, each with four bays. He rolled up the first door of the older building. Only three of the bays were occupied; the empty space was where his father's very first car used to sit. Now Dec saw it again, waxed to a glossy shine, the Wildcat. It was a black convertible with white interior. The top was down. He doubted his father had left it that way.

"Wish I'd known him when he was young," said Lindy.

Dec looked up. She had been standing in the shadows at the back of the garage, in a black raincoat with her collar up and the belt cinched tight. She looked like a spy.

"I was just out of school," she said. "He was thirty by then. Not so old, I guess, but some people age real fast."

She ran her hand admiringly along the chrome that stretched the length of the car and then leaned over to see her reflection in the hood.

"Think of it, Dec. Your daddy, just a boy, eighteen, away at college and—Pow!—both parents dead in a car crash." Her eyes flashed. "Suddenly he's a millionaire. Just like that! And the best part is, no meddling relatives to tell him what to do with his money."

She laughed out loud.

"I'd have said to hell with university if I'd been him, but not your dad, oh no." She scowled. "He was too busy majoring in boredom."

"Daddy's nice," Dec said.

"Oh, he's nice, all right," said Lindy. "Nice and handsome, nice and rich. Why else do you think a girl would marry a guy a dozen years older than her?"

"I don't know," said Dec, shoving his hands into his pockets. Adults all seemed about the same age to him.

Lindy scruffled his hair. "Bernard is so nice a girl could just die."

Dec wrapped his fists tightly around the MicroMachines in his pockets, a pickup in the left, an ambulance in the right.

"Ah, Skipper," she said, seeing the trouble in his eyes. "It's just that sometimes it seems like he's got his feet stuck in two big fat pails of concrete."

Dec laughed.

Then Lindy bent down so that they were eye to eye. "Do you ever ask yourself why?" she said, her voice a throaty whisper.

"Why what?"

"Why a guy like that would buy a car like this?"

Dec had never thought about it before. The Wildcat wasn't like any of his father's other cars, that was for sure.

She opened the driver's door and peered inside. "You know what I think? His folks dying like that so sudden must have scared some life into him." She made a face. "He sure got over it fast." She rubbed her hand over the leather of the driver's seat, shaking her head in wonder. Then she looked at Dec, a wicked grin on her face. "You think maybe he stole it?"

Dec laughed out loud. What a joke that was!

"Oh, ho!" she said. "You think your daddy never stole anything?" Her voice had changed. He couldn't tell anymore if she was fooling.

He kicked at the whitewalled tire. "Daddy's not a crook."

"Don't you be so sure," she said, wagging a finger at him. She held on to the car door and leaned way back.

"The man who bought this car was young and daring. When he showed it to me, I thought, Hey, girl—he may *seem* like a pussycat, driving his beige Le Sabre with the cruise control set right on the speed limit, but there's a *Wildcat* in there somewhere." Then she exploded with laughter. "Crazy mama," she said.

She grew quiet again and he watched, not sure what she would do next. Then the grin was back and she gave Dec a hurry-up wave. "Hop in, Big Stuff," she said. "Come on, quick now." He crawled in behind the steering wheel. She clambered over him and lounged in the passenger's seat. "Take me somewhere," she said.

"Where?" asked Dec, both hands on the wheel, only wishing that his foot could reach the pedal.

"California," said Lindy. "I need a little sun in my life. How 'bout you?"

He drove a bit. She made loud driving noises. She joked about him running over a cow. "Careful you don't put us in the river!" she said. "Hey, is that Las Vegas up ahead? I think it just might be. Viva Las Vegas!"

Then they sat quietly with only the sparkling green lawns of Steeple Hall before them. "You don't think your daddy was a crook?" she said, her voice tetchy now. "Well, I used to have a life. Where'd that go, huh?"

Dec sat staring at her, her bare feet up on the seat, her knees supporting her chin, her sad face, her puffy eyes. He didn't like it when she got sad. He crawled up on his knees, leaned over, and gave her a kiss on the cheek. She wrapped her arms around him.

"Get me out of here, Declan," she whispered between smooches. "Get me out of here. Before it's too late."

Thunder rumbled a long way off.

Dec opened his eyes. How old had he been? The memories came back to him willy-nilly. He had no control over them. Sometimes he was eight or nine, sometimes he was little more than a baby. But he never seemed to get too close in age to the time she left. That time was a blank. She had left in the fall, just a few months after Sunny was born. He had been ten.

He looked back toward the house. His ten-year-old self was walking around in there somewhere, lost to him.

Lightning crackled across the southern sky. He shuddered. He should go inside. He closed the door on the empty bay. The rain would be back, but the Wildcat wouldn't. One night she drove it away, all by herself.

PSYCHO

Dec had written about half his essay on Frank Lloyd Wright.

"Architecture as frozen music. I like that," said Ezra. "Is it about that place called Fallingwater?"

"The Edgar J. Kaufmann house," said Dec. "How do you know?"

"It's in Pennsylvania, right?" said Ezra. "I love it. All the angles and the way it sort of hangs out over the stream like that and . . ." He stopped. They had been making slow passage through the knot at the entrance to the cafeteria, but Ezra, who was taller than Dec, had his eyes on their table. "What's going on?" he said.

In truth, nothing was going on. Not the usual kind of thing anyway. Melody and Martin weren't at the blackboard solving the mysteries of the physical universe. Langston's chessboard was all set up but no one was playing. Arianna wasn't doing her crossword, and Vivien, back to regular clothing, if overalls and a fluorescent blue wig could be considered normal, was not composing in her journal. She looked anything but composed. She was tugging absent-mindedly at her eyebrow ring.

They were all crowded around something, their heads pressed together.

Vivien was the first to see the boys arrive. "Have you seen this?" she said to Dec.

The others cleared a path. What Dec saw was Steeple Hall. The image filled the top half of a page in some newspaper. The story filled the rest of the page. Under the picture, in large black letters, was the headline "A Thief in the House of Memory."

"Shit."

"It's the *Ottawa Citizen*," said Langston, hitching up his pants. "I went out to get a copy because I wrote this letter to the editor protesting the education cuts and it was supposed to be in today."

Speechless, Dec started to read the article.

In the countryside not far from the pretty town of Ladybank, a man died three weeks ago. He was a small-town crook crushed in his last act of larceny. He had tried to rob the House of Memory.

Dec tried to go on, but the words began to swim before his eyes.

"You didn't know about this?" asked Vivien.

He shook his head.

"Bummer," she said.

The house was shot from a distance but it still looked grotesquely tall, a lurid house of horrors. The image was grainy and distorted and they had used some kind of eerie effect to lend an artificial twilight to the scene.

"Ghost Central," said Richard.

Dec groaned. "Oh, perfect. This is just perfect."

"I wouldn't lose any sleep over it," said Arianna. She was sitting with the article in front of her and a yellow highlighter in her hand. "I've counted three typos so far." Dec stared at her vacantly. "Well, who is going to believe such shoddy journalism?"

"It's mostly about your grandfather," said Martin. "I didn't know he was a senator."

"That was his great-grandfather," said Melody.

"Oh, right. Your grandfather was the business guy."

"Steeple Industries," said Richard grandly, stretching out his arm as if pointing to a huge neon sign.

"Steeple *Enterprises*," corrected Langston. He turned to Dec. "Your family used to own half of Ladybank."

Dec had a sour taste in his mouth. "What's your point?" he snapped.

Langston shrugged. "I don't have a point."

"I read the article this morning," said Vivien hurriedly. "It's actually kind of inspiring."

Dec looked at her skeptically. "Really?"

"Really. It talks about how your dad has kind of appointed himself as the family historian, how committed he is, and how much work he puts into upkeep—that kind of thing."

Dec looked at the article and then back at Vivien hopefully.

"It's true," she said. "I even started writing a poem." She plunked her journal down on the table and started leafing through the pages. "It made me think of *The Fall of the House of Usher*. It's got this kind of Poe feel to it," she said. "So I call it a Poe-em."

As the journal pages flipped by, something caught Dec's eye, and he stopped her hand. A sketch—a good one—and it looked remarkably like him.

"Oh, that," she said. "Just a doodle." She snatched up the journal and held it to her chest. She pushed a strand of neon-blue hair from her face and cleared her throat.

"The Poe-em is written in trochaic octameter," she said.

"Is that some kind of dinosaur?" said Richard. But before Vivien could reply, Arianna made another mark with her yellow highlighter.

"Four!" she said triumphantly. "Can you believe they left out the *h* in 'psycho'?"

"Psycho?" said Dec, looking at her in shock. *"Psycho?"*

"It's okay," said Vivien, seeing the look of panic on Dec's face. "The journalist was just sort of saying something about the contrast between the . . . Here it is." She pointed to the passage and Dec read it for himself.

A lonely stretch of highway, a modest roadside dwelling at the foot of a steep hill leading, by a ragged pathway, to an imposing Victorian mansion. One might almost be describing the setting for Alfred Hitchcock's Psyco.

Dec smacked his forehead. "The setting for *Psycho!*"

"Keep reading," said Vivien.

But Dec's face was buried in his hands. "My father is going to freak."

"He must have known about it," said Martin.

"But he didn't," said Melody. "The journalist says that every attempt to contact Steeple was turned down."

"Then the guy was trespassing," said Martin. "You can sue!"

"Yeah, right," said Dec.

"It's defamation of character," said Richard. "Slander!"

"You mean libel," said Arianna. "When you actually *publish* a false statement, it's libel."

"Stop!" said Vivien with such passion that, remarkably, everybody did. "You have to read the whole thing, Dec. In the very next sentence he says . . . where is it . . . yeah, listen, 'Nothing could be further from the truth.' Then he goes on to say that your dad's this real family-minded guy who likes to live the quiet life and nice stuff like that."

Richard looked disappointed. "So your dad's not a psychotic killer?"

Dec looked at Richard wearily. "Richard, sometimes . . ."

"Hold on," said Ezra, interrupting. He stared at Dec, a

glint in his eye. "He asked you a question, Dec. Answer the guy."

Dec gaped at Ezra. And Ezra smiled back at him, but would not withdraw the challenge.

Dec swallowed hard. They were all looking at him now and waiting as if the question hadn't been a joke. "Is my dad a psychotic killer?" He fixed his eyes on Ezra. "The jury is still out."

THE PRICE OF FAME

A television van, with splashy call letters on its sides and a satellite dish on the roof, was parked outside Camelot. As the school bus pulled to a stop, the students went wild. Dec pushed his way through the crowd and down the steps.

The bus door closed behind him. The noise died to a dull roar and then was lost entirely under the din of the vehicle pulling away. It was raining lightly. A lady reporter headed toward Dec with a newspaper over her head for protection and a cameraman in tow. Bernard Steeple was trying to stop them.

"Get to the house!" he yelled. Dec froze.

"Just a word," said the reporter, bearing down on him. The gravel of the soft shoulder was hard going for her in heels.

"Don't say a thing!" Bernard yelled again. He grabbed the cameraman, who shook him off.

Dec had never seen his father like this.

"Move!"

Dec ran across the lawn toward the house. He glanced

back. The cameraman was filming him. Dec stopped. This was ridiculous. He felt like a criminal. Worse, he felt like some freak. What was he supposed to be running from?

"Just go!" shouted his father, waving his hands around as he stepped between Dec and the camera.

In the house, Dec locked the door but stood catching his breath, looking out the tiny window. He could hear the television in the rec room. *Reading Rainbow*. Sunny was home and, by the sound of it, oblivious to the commotion outside. Dec's eyes followed the trio on the lawn back toward the van.

It was only then that he noticed Birdie's black Beetle parked beside the Rendezvous.

She was sitting in the living room with a drink in her hand.

"What are you doing here?" he asked.

"I live here."

Dec lowered his head and sighed. "That isn't what I meant."

"I know," she said. "But you're not around much lately, so I thought, hey, I'd better remind you."

He tried again. "You're home early."

She nodded and peered toward the picture window. "The general was blowing a gasket. I figured I'd better call in Kerrie to hold the fort, and hustle my buns back here." She took another, longer swig of her drink. There was a bottle of Canadian Club on the coffee table.

Outside, the TV truck's horn sounded. Dec walked over

to the picture window to watch. The cameraman was behind the wheel, ready to go. The reporter handed Bernard
a business card. He accepted it with a stiff nod. He had
calmed down, but his shoulders were slumped. Dec looked
back at Birdie.

"Did he see the *Citizen* article?"

"Oh, yeah," she said. She patted the side of her hair,
found a loose strand, and had to put her drink down to pin
it back in place. "He had his lawyer on it right away. It
seems the photographer wasn't actually on the property, or
so he claims. He climbed a tree on the river road, used a
telephoto lens. There's some dispute about whether there's
still a public right of way on the old road. I don't know the
details and Frankly, Scarlett, I don't give a damn."

"But where'd they get all that information?"

She took another drink. "There's always someone in a
small town with a big mouth." She glanced at Dec and, as
quickly as she looked away, he saw the question in her eyes.

"You think I talked to them?"

She frowned and the makeup cracked around her
mouth. "I don't know what to think," she said. "And you
don't need to look at me like that. If you say you didn't,
that's good enough for me. It's just that lately you've been
kind of . . ."

"Kind of what?"

Her eyebrow arched. "Not exactly open, for starters."

Dec pulled a hassock over to the coffee table and sat

down. "*I'm* not very open?" he said. "I begged you guys to talk to me about the inquest and I got the cold shoulder."

She topped up her drink and leaned back heavily in her chair. "You're just spitting feathers," she said. "Why are you so angry?"

Dec shook his head. "So now this is my fault."

"Your father is beleaguered, Dec. That's the word he used—beleaguered. He needs our support. Can't you see that now is not the time for this?"

"This what?"

"This attitude, this moping around. This suspicion. You think we don't see it? What's it all about anyway? Where did it come from?" She leaned forward and poked the glass tabletop with her finger. "I'll tell you what I think. I think you've been spending way too much time up the hill."

Dec went cold. "What's that supposed to mean?"

She stirred her drink slowly with her finger. "You know what I'm saying: the House of Goddamned Memories." She shuddered. "That place gives me the creeps." Then she looked up at Dec, looked him square in the eye. "You thinking of moving up there?"

It was as if she had drawn a battle line in the sand. He wanted to move, all right. He wanted to stomp right out of the room and right out of Camelot and slam a few doors on the way. He noticed Birdie regarding him with an odd look in her eye—curious and anxious at the same time.

"You've been asking about Lindy," she said.

He nodded slowly. "What about it?"

She looked down at the bottle of rye, her gaze wavering. She didn't drink very often. He wondered if she was drunk. "It just seemed a little peculiar after so long," she said.

Dec couldn't keep the sarcasm out of his voice. "She *is* my mother," he said.

"And she *was* my best friend, okay? So don't get all high and mighty on me, Declan."

"All I did was ask Dad if she'd been in contact."

"Why?"

"Why not?"

"I mean, why *now*?" She swigged her drink without taking her eyes off him. "You've been skulking around. I wondered if you'd been doing a little eavesdropping."

Skulking? Eavesdropping? "What is it I'm supposed to have heard?"

She sighed and looked away, scratching distractedly at the skin above the top button of her blouse. She tanned at a parlor all winter and her skin was orangey-colored.

"Birdie?"

She was staring at nothing, but he had the feeling she was thinking hard about something. Then she reached a decision. "I guess you might as well hear it from me as anyone. Your dad and I are talking about getting married."

It took him a moment to figure out what she was saying. "But that's impossible."

"Gee, thanks."

"Dad's still married—to Lindy."

Birdie's eyes grew wide. "Really? I hadn't noticed."

"You know what I mean."

The mockery went out of her eyes. She looked down into her glass. It was empty. "Oh, I know what you mean, all right," she said bitterly. She placed her glass on the coffee table. It clinked on the glass top. She reached for a coaster and placed the glass on it. Dec stared out the window. His father was walking past the house toward his shop, back to that other war—the one he could handle. Dec's gaze returned to Birdie. Her eyes were bleary—from drink, or was she crying?

"You caught me off guard," he said. "I just . . ."

"Just wondered why your dad would want to bother marrying little old me?"

"That's not what I was going to say."

"Not exactly a beauty queen, like your mom."

"It isn't that," he said. "I just didn't think you could get divorced if the other person didn't know about it." Then a new idea struck him like a lightning bolt. "*Does* she know?" he asked. "Has he talked to her?"

"No!" snapped Birdie. Then she rubbed her forehead. "No," she repeated more quietly. "He has not talked to her and, as you can see, she is most certainly *not* around."

She stood up, a little wobbly on her feet, and looked at him with barely concealed resentment. He had hurt her feelings and he wasn't sure how.

"I'll tell you something else for free," she said. "She is not ever going to be around, Dec. Get used to it. So you don't need to sound so all-fired hopeful." Then she picked up her glass and headed toward the kitchen.

Through the sheer curtains of the bay window, Dec saw his father reappear with his red tool kit. He crossed the road and started to take down the House of Memory mailbox. The rain wasn't hard but it was steady; soon he was drenched. Finally, the job was done and Bernard hoisted the thing up in one arm, his tool kit in the other.

He looked both ways before crossing the road, the way he had taught Dec when he was little. Then he marched across County Road 10 and around the side of the house to his workshop.

Your dad and I are talking about getting married.

Why was it such a shock? They had been together pretty much since Lindy left. Birdie had been Lindy's friend. He hadn't really forgotten that. She had been the first to comfort Bernard in his loss—in their mutual loss. Comfort had turned to helping out with baby Sonya. And helping out had led eventually to moving in, which had led not much later to Camelot. She had never liked the big house.

Dec leaned his forehead on the window glass. *Talking about getting married.* So was that what all the whispering was about? Was that why his dad looked so guilty?

He looked back toward the road. The headless black post upon which the mailbox had stood looked like one of the mines on his father's model beach. The beach codenamed Love. Dec's eyes wandered to the rough ground beyond the post. There was an old split-rail fence choked with wild grape. Through a gap in it, a path meandered down to a creek. A memory stirred in him.

It was after Sunny was born, a kinder, warmer day than this one. He had taken her in her Snugli down to the creek to look at the tadpoles. He was heading home again when he saw his mother coming down the long drive from Steeple Hall. There was no Camelot then, just an unassuming dirt driveway that might have looked to a passerby like a road to an orchard or a cottage. They were heading toward each other, Dec up from the creek, Lindy down from the house, with only the county road between them.

But she didn't see him. She was kind of hurrying and looking back over her shoulder, wearing tight jeans and her suede jacket, the one with the eight-inch fringe along the arms and the Indian embroidery on the pockets.

He was going to shout to her, but Sunny was sleeping. So he just waited for her to notice them. She didn't. She got to the road and threw out her thumb. He felt torn. She was right there not fifty feet away, but she was hitching. Why? Was Daddy too busy to take her where she wanted to go? Then he thought, it doesn't matter, and he was about to go to her anyway, when a car came from the west heading toward town.

Just like that.

Almost as if she had timed it.

ALARM

It wasn't until the next day that Dec could get his father alone. He arrived home from school to find the house empty and made his way to the shop. It was empty as well, apart from the miniature troops crowding the worktable: Brits, Yanks, Canucks. They were all lined up and ready, painted and waiting. On the beach, the Nazis were waiting, too, sandbagged and camouflaged, dressed in *Feldgrau*— field gray. His father had talked about it all through dinner last night. He'd talked about all sorts of things—anything he could think of that wasn't anything at all.

Dec found him, at last, up at the House of Memory. The front door was wide open and he was in the vestibule with his tool kit and the packaging for a security system. He was attaching the alarm keypad to the wall and didn't hear Dec arrive over the sound of the drill. He startled when he saw him.

"Thought you might be the man from the phone company," he said. "We're going to have to get the line reconnected."

Dec stood at the threshold. "Birdie says you're getting married."

His father carried on with his task. The drill whirred; another screw sank home. He spoke calmly but firmly. "She spoke out of turn," he said.

"So you're not getting married?"

The drill whirred again. Stopped. Bernard stepped back to inspect his work. "We're looking into an annulment."

"What's that?"

"A judicial proceeding to nullify the marriage. That's all."

That's all, thought Dec. Declare the marriage null, as if it never happened. He leaned against the doorframe. "Does Lindy know?"

His father looked cross. "Lindy was beyond caring about any of us a very long time ago."

"You know that for a fact?" demanded Dec. "She told you that?"

"No," said his father. "How many times do I have to tell you, son? I have not heard from her. Period." With a weary sigh he sat down on the pew. He bent over his drill, removing the Phillips head bit, putting it back in its case. Then he carefully placed the case back in the neatly appointed tool kit. He looked up at Dec, squinting a bit from the sun. "What's all this about?"

Dec shifted his weight to the other leg. What was it about?

"Birdie has been good to you," said his father patiently.

"She's been a mother for Sonya, who never really knew Lindy. And as for me, where am I likely to find another woman her equal?"

Not in your workshop, Dec thought. Not unless you send away to a model company. Maybe you could get someone in 1:72 scale.

He wanted to say that, but he held his tongue.

"Dec, do you have a problem with this?"

Dec shook his head. But he did, he did have a problem. Lindy. Her memory, buried for so long, had burst out of him like a jack-in-the-box, demanding his attention. She was everywhere, especially up here.

"It's just that Mom . . . never . . ."

But he wasn't sure what Mom never did. Never said goodbye?

"I'm listening," said his father.

But for some reason Dec didn't want to share his thoughts with his father. Didn't want to share Lindy with him.

"Is this about the estate?"

Dec's head jerked back. "What?"

"Is that what's on your mind?" said his father. "Because the estate is not an issue. It will be settled on you and Sunny. That's the way it was always going to be. Birdie knows that."

Dec's face puckered with distaste. "I don't care about the money," he said. "And I sure as hell don't care about this place." It wasn't what he meant to say, not really, but he couldn't take it back.

His father replaced the portable drill in its case and snapped the lid shut. He looked up, his face a mask. "Well, that's useful to know," he said.

He looked past Dec down the hill. He frowned and glanced at his wrist, which was bare, though the skin was pale where his watch should have been.

"What happened to your watch?"

His father looked at him, still frowning and looking a little pained. "I broke it," he said. Then he picked up his tool kit and squeezed past Dec out the door.

"How?"

His father stopped on the porch and turned slowly back. "How what?"

"How'd you break your watch?"

His father's hurt expression deepened. "I don't understand."

"It's a simple question, Dad. A guy wears a watch every day, then suddenly he's not wearing it."

His father glanced again at his wrist. "I broke it when I was building the wall in my shop. Okay? Why do you want to know?"

Dec rubbed his face. "Forget it," he said. But the expression in his father's eyes said he wouldn't forget it any time soon.

With one last worried glance back at Dec, he left. Dec

watched him until he had disappeared over the lip of the hill. Then he closed the door and leaned his forehead against it, his eyes closed. In the dark of his mind he saw his father, his hand grasping the neck of a bronze head. He saw him raise the thing high in the air and bring it down with such force on the back of Dennis Runyon's head that the watch on his father's arm flew apart. He opened his eyes with a start.

A rattling sound interrupted his thoughts. It came from inside. He listened, heard a low murmuring: Lindy talking to herself. Or so he thought. Then he wondered if she was talking to someone else, though no one answered her. He peered through the crack of the vestibule door.

She was in the front hall—standing on a stepladder in her flouncy wedding dress and a black cowboy hat. The ladder was near the bookcase. She must have been kneeling on the topmost step because the chiffon of the dress fell down around the ladder, making it look as if she had absurdly long, aluminum legs. He almost laughed but stopped himself. He was upset with her. Why hadn't she come to meet the bus? She always met him at the bottom of the hill. What was she doing up on a ladder talking to herself?

Then he realized she was talking to one of the busts that stood on the top of the bookcases. She was eye to eye with it—the one with the broken nose and the scowling face. She had one hand on the shelf for balance; the other hand was stroking the bronze head. She was so close—whispering close—and it almost looked to Dec as if she was going to kiss it.

"Mom?"

She jerked her hands away and teetered on her perch.

"Mom!" he cried, afraid she was going to fall.

"Dec," she said when she had recovered her balance. She clambered down the steps and turned to him, brushing her hands together, rubbing them down the front of her dress. "Jeez, you scared me! Is it so late?"

"What were you doing?"

Her eyes grew large, as if she was holding back a joke. She looked up at the bust and then back at Dec. "I was sharing a little secret with Mr. Know-it-all," she said at last.

Dec looked up at the grim face. "What secret?" he asked.

She came and gave him a brisk hug and a smacking great kiss right on the top of his head.

"It wouldn't be a secret if I told you," she said brightly. She rubbed at the fingers of her right hand. They were grimy, but the substance came off easily enough in rubbery strands.

"Tell me," he said.

She put her hands on her hips as if she was angry. "So now I've got two men around the house I have to answer to," she said, tapping her foot. "And all the time I thought you were on my side."

"I am," he said. "Tell me what the secret is."

The cowboy hat was a child's thing with a string under the chin to hold it in place. There was a black-and-white whistle attached to the end of the string. Lindy put the whistle between her lips and blew three times. Dec stepped back, covering his ears.

"Oh, sorry," she said. "I thought you were deaf."

"I'm not deaf."

"Well, then don't keep asking me what the secret is. It's private. A girl's got to have some privacy. Don't you think?"

He nodded, but he was confused. Didn't she trust him anymore? "I never tell Daddy any of our secrets," he said. "Honest."

She smiled and made a kissy face. "I know you don't, Skipper." Her hands cradled his face. She smoothed back his hair. "My, my," she said, combing it out with her fingers. She took it in her hands on either side of his head and pulled it out like bird's wings. She pulled and pulled.

"Owww!"

She stopped and leaned forward until she was eye to eye with him. "A boy should *never* have so much hair a girl can pull it," she said.

Through the tears in his eyes, he gazed at the expectant look on her face. He knew what that meant.

"Time to get scalped?" he said.

"And who scalps Chief Big Hair?"

"Birdie does."

"And who is Birdie?"

"The bestest friend a girl ever had?"

"You got it, Skipper."

She held him close. The bodice of her dress felt crinkly and stiff against his cheek. It smelled old. He pulled away from her and she pouted.

"You don't love me anymore," she said. And before he could say a word—before he could say that he loved her more than anything in the world—she found her whistle again and started blowing it, so shrill and loud Dec had to wrap his arms around his head. His eyes filled with fresh tears and he yelled at her to stop, but she just kept blowing till her face was as red as her hair.

FUTURE PERFECT

Dec stared across Forester Street at the freshly painted facade of Birdie's Hair Ideas. There was a new logo painted on the plate glass, a chirpy bird sitting on the busty upper loop of the *B* looking as if it had just escaped from *Snow White*. Through the window he saw a customer pay Birdie at her desk by the door. The woman stopped to admire her new do in the storefront glass, tapping the bird on its cute little beak as she walked by. There was no one else in the salon.

As he crossed Forester, Dec felt he could still hear Lindy blowing her toy whistle in his ear. He turned, expecting to catch a glimpse of her following him, spying on him.

A bell jingled as he opened the door. There was new country playing on the radio and Birdie was humming along as she swept up.

"Hey, Dec," she said, cheerily enough. Then she looked at the clock on the wall—another bird, this one bright blue and electric. "You're a little early if you're looking for a ride."

He glanced around the salon, so familiar to him, but different from the one he was remembering right now. He placed his backpack by the low table littered with magazines. The room he remembered was bigger. Or was that just because he had been so much smaller?

"Something the matter?" she asked.

"Was it here Mom used to bring me?"

Birdie frowned. "What is this, National Lindy Polk Month?"

Dec ignored the crack. "I remember lots of gold."

Birdie looked wary. "That would've been Mimi's Cut 'n Curl," she said. "Up on Dunlop. Least it used to be. She closed up shop a while back."

Dec sat down on a cream-colored Naugahyde chair, felt the cool vinyl surface with his hand. The waiting room chairs at Mimi's had been gold. "Mimi, was she the tubby one with the sparkly hair?"

Birdie smiled despite herself. "You got her."

Dec smiled, too. "She used to give me Tootsie Rolls," he said.

Surprise brought on another smile. "Tootsie Rolls was how she got so tubby," she said, leaning on her broom. "But that was a long time ago. I'm amazed you can remember."

Dec was amazed, too. "All those women. They were all over me. Scared me to death."

Birdie laughed. "You were a cute little tyke."

"But I was promised to you, right?" he said. " 'The bestest friend a girl ever had.' "

For a fleeting instant Birdie looked overcome with sadness. Then her expression changed. She looked kind of guilty, as if she had been scolded. "If it sounded like I was bad-mouthing Lindy the other day," she said, "it was just the whiskey talking. You've got to know that."

"You didn't bad-mouth her."

"Didn't I?" She shook her head as if she really couldn't remember. "I guess I just feel like I did. Left a bad taste in my mouth. Anyway, I'm sorry. It didn't go so well, eh?"

"It was a bad day all 'round."

She nodded, but looked only vaguely relieved. "Maybe seeing your dad in such a state reminded me of what it got to be like with them. I loved that girl, you know, but she could drive a man crazy."

Is that what had happened? Had Lindy driven Bernard crazy? *Get me out of here, Declan, before it's too late.* Did she really just run off and leave Dec behind, or did she *have* to go—running for her life?

Birdie put aside her broom and came toward him. He couldn't read her eyes but they looked filled with purpose. She stopped across the low table from him and her resolve seemed to abandon her. She smoothed out her tight skirt, straightened her belt.

"You were going to say something. Something about Lindy."

"No," she said. "I was just caught up in . . . in remembering."

"What happened, Birdie? Something happened."

She came around the table and stood above him. Hesitantly, she touched his unruly hair. Her fingers caught in a snag. He pulled his head away.

"There are women who'd kill for hair this shade," she said.

He pushed the hair out of his eyes. "You told me once I looked like an Irish setter who'd been playing in a briar patch."

She smiled, but her gaze was distant.

"Birdie, please. Something's going on. I can see it in your eyes."

Again, she looked as if she was about to speak and stopped herself. "Nothing's going on," she said more forcefully now. "It's just you."

Dec threw himself against the back of the chair.

"Don't get your shorts in a knot," she said. "It's just seeing you, right now. I mean, really *seeing* you. I'm so used to thinking of you as Bernard's son, I forget how much like her you are."

He swallowed the lump in his throat. "I don't have her hair."

She took a balled-up tissue from her pocket and dabbed at the corner of her eyes. "Sunny got the hair, all right," she said. "But you got her eyes. That kind of blue with just enough hazel in them to make a person look twice." She looked a little bashful. And then, suddenly, overwrought. "And you've got that kind of accusing look she used to throw around when things weren't going her way."

"Thanks," he said.

"Just so you know."

With a little shudder, she seemed to recover from whatever reflection or memory had held her in its grip. "You even sound like her," she said. "Funny how I never noticed before." She looked thoughtful.

Dec shrugged. "Sometimes I think I can hear her—I mean, remember her voice. Do I really sound like her?"

Birdie perched on the seat beside him, her knees pressed tightly together. She brushed lint from her skirt.

"It's not your voice so much as the kind of things you say. Lindy couldn't wait to get out of here. Just like you. For her, everything happened too slow."

Too slowly, he thought, but he kept it to himself. "Maybe she was just bored."

"I remember the day after her fifteenth birthday she started telling everyone she was sixteen. I said to her, 'Lindy Polk, you're a damn liar.' And she said, 'BV, I am now officially in my sixteenth year.' "

"You were really close," said Dec.

"I remember this other time," said Birdie, barreling on. "It was right after English class and she said, 'BV, finally we learned something worthwhile.' I asked her what that might be, and she said, 'The future perfect. Now there's a tense a girl could get to love.' "

"There's no way she would have just forgotten you," said Dec.

"She wanted the world and she wanted it on the double, please and thank you."

"She would have at least let you know where she was," said Dec.

Birdie was staring—not at him, not at anything. He held his breath. On the country station, somebody was leaving somebody, but that was always happening in country songs.

Finally her eyes focused again. She sighed. "She did *not* tell me where she was going," she said. "Lindy was *always* going and leaving a mess behind. I spent half my life picking up after that girl."

Then Birdie rose, found the dustpan and brush, and finished sweeping up.

"The thing I could never understand was that she saw perfectly clearly what your dad was like. She saw how kind and gentle he was, how *settled* he was. But she thought she could change him anyway." She swept a bit and stopped. "Well, she changed him all right."

"What do you mean?"

"She hurt him bad."

"Maybe he hurt her."

Birdie glanced at him unsmilingly. "I don't want to hear that kind of talk," she said, and went to put the broom away.

When she returned, Dec said, "I didn't mean he hurt her on purpose. It was just his lifestyle. She thought there was going to be more."

Birdie nodded and looked down at her shoes. "She sure never dreamed she was going to rot away in a huge empty house in the middle of nowhere."

Dec thought about it a moment. Then he nodded. "So I guess it all worked out in the end," he said. "She got away and you got Dad and everybody's happy."

He wasn't sure what it was about this simple summary that made the tears well in Birdie's eyes. "If only that were true," she said. Then with one last look around to make sure her little kingdom was tidy, she headed to the back room for her coat, sobbing the whole way.

THE HOUSE OF STONE

The house looks like Steeple Hall, but when he opens the great front door the interior is made entirely of stone. The Oriental rug in the hall is stone, the stairs are stone, the chandelier is stone. Even the keypad of the new alarm by the vestibule door is made of stone. He punches in the code numbers, which he knows somehow. He makes his way down the front hall toward his grandfather's study. The corridor is a great deal longer than he remembers it being, and it's tilted so that he feels all the time as if he's falling.

Falling into the dark.

What light there is comes from thin cracks between the great slabs of polished granite. Above his head, statues stare down at him from the top of stone bookcases.

"Lindy?" he calls, and his voice echoes all around him.

It is so cold that he shivers uncontrollably. He is in his pajamas. He wishes he had thought to dress warmly. He wishes he did not feel so alone. He wishes he had never set out on this journey.

He hears whispering and follows the sound.

"Mom?" he calls.

The whispering grows until it seems to engulf him. Finally he stands outside a door to a room he did not know was there. He tries the handle but it will not budge. He presses his ear against the cold polished surface. He hears his father's voice.

"Lindy was beyond caring long ago."

He hears whispering farther down the corridor. At another door he stops to listen.

"She never dreamed she was going to rot away in a huge empty house in the middle of nowhere."

He moves on.

"Dec?" someone calls. "Dec!" He runs until he comes, at last, to the door at the very end of the corridor.

"Mom?" he whispers.

"Dec," she says breathlessly. "Get me out of here, before it's too late."

THE HOLE IN THE WALL

Not many kids hung out at the Hole in the Wall. Dec and Ezra liked it for the salt and pepper shakers. Each table boasted a different set. In the corner booth where Ezra was sitting, the saltshaker was a fat lady in a dressing gown with her hair up in curlers. The pepper shaker was a refrigerator with the door open. The little ceramic saltshaker lady had her hands on her hips and she looked as if she was trying to decide on a midnight snack.

When Dec entered the café, Ezra was intently looking over the painted contents of the refrigerator.

"She should definitely go for the cake," said Ezra.

Dec plumped himself down across from him. He had a bundle of mail wrapped up in a thick rubber band. "Dad's taken out a post office box until the 'media blitz' is over," he said. "You'd think he was Michael Jackson or something."

"It's a Thriller day in the neighborhood," sang Ezra.

Dec cast him a scornful glance. "The Mr. Rogers thing is getting pretty old," he said.

Ezra looked over the top of his glasses. "Did somebody miss his nap?"

Dec wasn't in the mood for jokes. He slipped off the rubber band and flipped through the letters. Only the magazine at the bottom of the pile interested him, the latest issue of *Architectural Record*. There was a house on the cover that looked as if a forest was growing inside it. He thumbed through the pages.

"I thought this was urgent," said Ezra.

Dec paused when he saw the reminder of the student design contest—"The Shape of Things to Come." He closed the magazine and stared dejectedly at his friend.

Ezra cleared his throat. "Has anyone told you yet today that you look like refried dog food?"

"Thanks for noticing."

The waitress came and Dec ordered an Orangina. Ezra had already ordered a carrot muffin and a cappuccino. The drink sat before him in a bowl the size of a birdbath. He held it with two hands and took a long, noisy sip. Dec winced.

Ezra said, "Either you've got a hangover or things are not good on the annulment front."

Dec shook his head. "That's old news," he said. The annulment now seemed like the least of his worries. But how would Ezra know? There was too much Ezra *didn't* know. That was the problem. He had to tell him about his dream—he had to tell someone. But in order to do that, he had to start a long way back.

"I've been seeing a lot of my mother lately," he said. Then he launched in, not caring if he sounded like a raving lunatic. He clammed up when the waitress brought his order and started up again as soon as she was out of earshot. He poured out everything and felt his loneliness drain out of him as well.

When he was done, he gulped down some Orangina, concentrating on the act as if drinking soda required a lot of serious attention. But he was also avoiding Ezra's gaze. That was the trouble with spilling your guts: you felt exposed, stupid. Finally he dared to look up, and Ezra was waiting for him.

"You're not crazy," he said. "Well, maybe a little crazy, but not beyond help."

"Thanks, Doc," said Dec.

"All part of the friendly service," said Ezra. "The thing is, I've been thinking and I realized something. That big old house of yours is one giant mnemonic device. It's like a memory-making assembly line. Remember that *I Love Lucy* show where she's working on the assembly line and she can't keep up?" Dec nodded. "Maybe there's such a thing as too many memories."

"What am I supposed to do?"

"I guess it would be pretty hard to talk to your dad, huh?"

"What am I supposed to say? 'Uh, Pops, I was just wondering. Did you by any chance kill Mom?' "

"I see your problem."

Dec rested his head on his arms and closed his eyes. He was so sleepy. He had woken from last night's nightmare in the clutches of an inescapable certainty. It had all seemed to make terrifying sense. He had lain in his bed panic-stricken, scarcely able to breathe. Then Sunny had started fussing—her ear again. Birdie had gotten up to comfort her, and Dec had drifted off to sleep finally, only to be awakened at the usual hour by "Hit the deck, Dec."

The dream was so horrific, the reality so banal. Where did the truth lie?

He opened his eyes. Ezra was observing him closely.

"What about motive?" he said. "Your mother sounds totally nuts to me. But you don't kill someone just because she's nuts."

"Maybe it was accidental."

"Like the 'accidental' death of Dennis Runyon?"

Dec swallowed hard. "Maybe I am crazy after all. Maybe I caught it from my mom."

Ezra got a thoughtful look in his black crow eyes. "Think of the dream. Forget the other stuff for the moment. What does the dream tell you?"

"That my mother is dead," said Dec. "That my dad and Birdie both knew about it. That maybe he killed her or maybe they both did, and buried her in the House of Memory."

"Okay. So your mother is dead. What does that mean?"

Dec looked confused.

"It's a dream, Dec. It's not literally true. Read between the lines."

Dec thought about it. "That my mother is . . . dead." He shook his head. "Sorry, Ezra, but I'm kind of brain-dead myself."

"Okay, let me throw on my Cling Wrap hat here and try an idea on you. If you think about it, your mother *is* dead in a way, isn't she? You haven't seen her—really seen her—for years. You didn't think about her much, as far as I know, until this happened. All I knew was that she wasn't around anymore."

Dec's brow knotted. "So you're saying the dream was just me admitting something to myself?"

"A delayed reaction."

"Delayed a long time."

Ezra shrugged. "Grief is like that. My bubby said she didn't really mourn Zaida's death for ten years. Then one day it just came over her—Whoosh!"

Dec smiled wistfully. "Maybe you *should* be a shrink," he said.

Ezra frowned. "I think I'll stick to physics. Subatomic particles are weird enough."

Dec felt utterly exhausted. "I feel like somebody's holding me by the legs and shaking and shaking and shaking, and all this crap is coming out of me. I just wish I knew what to do."

Ezra peered at Dec, his eyes narrowed behind his tiny

glasses. "You need to separate the data from the interpretation."

"What data? There's nothing here you could call evidence. Just memories stirred up by a very bad feeling in my gut."

Ezra nodded. "Have you ever thought of looking for her?"

Dec stared at him dumbly. "My mother?"

"No, Dec. Amelia Earhart."

"Look where? She hasn't written since March 8, 1998."

Ezra began typing on the tabletop.

"The Internet?"

Ezra nodded and then, as if his work was over, he took a big bite out of his muffin.

Dec looked down at the table, surprised that he had never thought of it. He wrapped his arms around himself. Did he really want this?

Meanwhile, the architecture magazine on the table diverted his attention. A house with trees growing inside it; or was it a grove of trees that a house had grown up around? It was brilliant. It elated him—the magic of it. Then it made him ache inside so much he had to hold his stomach. He turned the magazine over.

"I'll never be an architect," he said.

"That's true," said Ezra with his mouth full.

Dec's head snapped back. "You missed your cue," he said. "This is where a best friend says, 'Sure you will, old buddy, old pal.' "

Ezra swallowed and wiped the crumbs off his mouth. "Ah, but we have a different sense of what 'I' means. You think of 'I' as part of a continuum, the locus of which you call Declan Steeple."

"Now I'm a locust? Thanks a lot."

"A locus, Dec. A set of points, the position of which—"

"Cut to the chase, Dr. Harlow."

"I'm talking about how a person is really a succession, a series of selves. These selves are connected in what *seems* to be a unique and discrete entity by a mysterious but nonetheless quantifiable link called the andthen."

"Andthen?"

"Exactly. And your dream of becoming an architect is still a couple of andthens away."

Dec grinned. "So, you're saying I'm a *couple* of andthens short of a load?"

"Well, three actually," said Ezra, looking thoughtful. He lined up the sugar bowl and what was left of his muffin beside his half-finished bowl of coffee. "This is andthen number one," he said, touching the coffee bowl. "This is andthen number two and number three," he said, opening his hands above the sugar bowl and the muffin in the manner of a magician indicating a couple of rabbits he has just pulled from a hat.

"Great," said Dec. "My future is a half-eaten muffin?"

Ezra smiled condescendingly. "Work with me, Dec. This coffee cup is andthen number one: that would be the rest of your secondary school education. The sugar bowl is andthen number two: college. Which brings us, finally, to andthen number three: international acclaim. Ta da!"

Dec's eyes wandered back to the coffee bowl. The contents looked tepid and unappetizing. This was now? He picked up the saltshaker and plunked it down beside the coffee bowl. "You forgot something," he said. "I've still got this to deal with."

Ezra stared at the lady in her dressing gown and rollers with her hands on her hips and the perplexed look on her face. "Ah, yes," he said. "That messy midnight marauder, the past."

STEALING BACK THE PAST

There was a missing persons cybercenter. There were missing persons help-lines, message boards, registers, indexes, and clearing houses. There were missing Irish people and missing Yugoslavian people. Lots of missing Yugoslavian people. There were kidnappings and unidentified bodies and unsolved mysteries and fugitives.

Dec surfed aimlessly for hours. Where to begin?

With a photo of Lindy. He could post it online. And he knew where to find one, even though it would mean going back up to the big house.

He made his way upstairs to the room with *Lindy* on the door. He opened it, stood on the threshold.

There wasn't much there. She had never lived in this room. It had been a place for her to hang her clothes, play her guitar, write her songs. The guitar was long since gone, one of the few things she bothered to take with her. There were photo albums on a bookshelf along with her high school yearbooks and a few romance novels. He sorted through the photographs, found himself trembling a little, hurrying. He picked what he needed, then closed the drawer. He should go—go right away. But it was too late.

He heard his name being called. The voice seemed to come from far away. He looked around in alarm before crossing the room and looking out the window.

She stood on the back lawn by a birch tree, beckoning him. She was wearing a short, cotton-print summer dress with spaghetti straps. She was shoeless. By the time he had made his way outside, she was at the far end of the garden. There were steps cut into the steep bank leading down to the Eden River. She disappeared down the hill. He ran after her, tumbling down the steps like a bruised-knee child, laughing at the headlong speed of his descent. As soon as he reached the bottom, he gathered a pile of lumber: scraps of two-by-fours and offcuts of plywood, a few cedar logs. He had a big wooden-handled hammer from his grandfather's workshop and jars of the biggest nails he could find. He was building a raft.

"Now, that's some boat." She was squatting on the last earthen step. "You reckon that thing could take us out to sea?"

He stopped hammering and looked at his handiwork. He shrugged. "Maybe as far as the Tay."

"Good enough," said Lindy. "The Tay connects up to the Rideau, doesn't it? Then there's the canal to the Saint Lawrence, and after that you're laughing. Next stop gay Paree."

Dec looked out at the lazy river. All he wanted the raft to do was float. If he could pole his way across to the other bank, that would be something. There was an apple orchard there he could plunder like a pirate. But Lindy wanted so much more.

"Build me a boat that will carry two, and both shall row, my love and I." It was one of the songs she played on the guitar, but not as much lately. The guitar didn't seem to take her where she wanted to go, either.

A noise made him look up from his work. It was over in the bushes where the old road was. A rustling, that was all. Then a glimpse of something moving, something brown.

"A deer," said Lindy. Her eyes were smiling. "Did you see it, Dec?" He wasn't sure what he saw. "A buck," she said. "He was beautiful. We'll tell Daddy we saw a buck." Her eyes grew large. "Let's say it was a giant buck with huge antlers, each with a hundred points on it."

"Daddy gets mad when we make up stories," he said.

"I know," said Lindy, beaming.

Now Dec sat on the same earthen step. He closed his eyes and a sense of uneasiness claimed him. The ground was damp. It was cold in the deep shade. A deer. Had there been a deer? Night was coming on. He climbed to his feet and headed back up the earthen stairs. He stopped and looked down at the riverside.

He *had* made her a boat of some kind. A birthday present. It came back to him but not clearly. His memories, so crystal clear one moment, were disjointed, fragmented the next. Had he made the boat or had he only thought of making it?

There was one way to find out. Back in the room with *Lindy* on the door, there was a shelf on which were arrayed, like trophies, all the presents he had made for her: things of paper, things of felt, and things of string and pipe cleaners. The ashtray with notes painted on it, a little house made of offcuts from his grandfather's lathe. But no boat.

"Deckly Speckly?"

He jumped at the sound of Sunny's voice. She was standing at the door.

"What are you doing here?" he snapped. He saw her flinch, her lip quiver. "Sorry," he said. "You just caught me by surprise."

She looked miserable. "Daddy said I could come Up 'cause your Note said you were Here and the alarm system isn't turned On yet. He said when the 'larm system Is on I won't be able to Come here anymore on my own Because I'm Too Small. I couldn't find you, but I stayed anyway because you know Why?"

"Why?"

"I miss my Polly Pockets." She said it so sadly he was afraid she was going to cry.

He looked at her tenderly. She was wearing her yellow raincoat with a green cardigan under it, and she had a bandage over her ear. They had gone to see the doctor.

He squatted and she came to him. He gave her a hug. "What's this?" he said. He gently pushed her away until she was at arm's length. Then he smiled. Every available pocket was stuffed with tiny dolls.

She tried to cover them up. Her brow furrowed.

"Daddy will be mad," she said.

Dec grinned with complicity. "He won't be mad if he doesn't know." Sunny smiled, and it was Lindy's smile, devilish and one hundred watts strong.

"Let's go," she said, and ran to the grand stairway. But when she got there she wanted Dec to go ahead of her. He waited obediently at the foot of the stairs. He looked up and watched her mount the wide, smooth oak rail, watched her hug it to her chest. She didn't slow herself at all as she came hurtling down the graceful curve until she flew into his arms, knocking him clear over.

She roared with laughter and flung herself back spread-eagle on the carpet. Dec laughed, too, until it occurred to him that his sister was lying exactly where Dennis Runyon had fallen.

"Come on," he said, holding out his hand. "Dec has work to do."

Sunny didn't take his hand. She was gazing up at the bust on the bookcase. "Hello, Mr. Play-Doh," she said, pushing great gobs of hair from her eyes. "Sorry we don't get a chance to Talk no more."

Dec looked at the statue. He saw his mother perched on the ladder, eye to eye with it. What was she doing? *I was sharing a little secret with Mr. Know-it-all,* she had said.

"Anymore," he said distractedly, and he took Sunny's

hand to pull her up. She leaped into his arms and wrapped her legs around him.

"*Any*more," she said.

"You're too old for this," he complained. "You're too heavy."

Sunny threw her head back and laughed. One of her Polly Pockets fell out. She jumped down to retrieve it and shoved it back in her pocket. " 'Member, Deckly, Don't Tell." She put her finger to his lips. He pretended to bite her finger. But she was serious. "Daddy doesn't like it when we Take stuff out of the Big House. Once it's Here, it's a Memory, right?"

"Take whatever you like," said Dec.

"Somebody else is," she said.

Dec was busy locking the front door. "Is what?"

"Taking stuff!"

"Like what?"

She looked at him as if he was setting a trap. "In Lindy's room," she said. "I wanted to look at that yearbook, the One where she's Queen of the Pumpkin Patch. Birdie showed it to Me a Long time ago. But It wasn't There."

"Are you sure?" he said.

She glared at him. "Course I'm sure. Three books are there. One is Gone."

A BOAT FULL OF NAILS

Dec went back up to the big house later that evening. The trees were full of rain. The moon, between the clouds, seemed to sputter and flare like a candle in a drafty room. He followed the meager path of his flashlight up the hill. Then he made his way through the house, turning lights on as he went. Through the dining hall—*Click*. The arched and narrow corridor that led to the vast kitchen—*Click*. Left to the pantry—*Click*. Left again to the servants' entrance— *Click*. Left a third time to the cellar door. *Click*.

The stairs were steep. They creaked under his weight. At the bottom he pulled a string and a bare bulb glowed, though not nearly bright enough in the crowded darkness. The cellar was really several connected cellars, floored here in cement and there in brick and, in the oldest reaches, nothing more than compacted earth.

She is not ever going to be around, Dec. Get used to it. He grabbed hold of the stair rail. He tried to remember Ezra's comforting voice explaining away his mad thoughts.

The heart of the cellar, where he now stood, was ruled

by a giant oil furnace that reminded him of some medieval torture chamber. It was no longer in use. His father had put in an efficient electric furnace some years back, but he had left the old iron monstrosity in its place, part of his private museum.

Stooping under the old ductwork, Dec made his way down a corridor crowded by wide shelves lined with cloudy pickle jars and ancient dark jars of fruit preserve. This was the way. *Click.* The deeper he went the less adequate the light seemed. The ceiling was lower, the walls and cupboards closed in around him. There was a smell of dampness and rot.

His grandfather's old shop was under the newer east wing. There were steps down, just a couple, but they allowed some headroom, some breathing room. The worktable stood against the farthest wall of the room, beyond the perimeter of the light. Dec made his way toward it, holding his breath and staring into every shadowy corner. He reached for the string above the bench. *Click.*

He had loved this worktable. He couldn't remember the last time he'd been down here. The bench was exactly as he recalled it except for a blanket of dust. But there was no boat. He must only have imagined making it. And yet . . .

He scanned the work top. Nothing was out of place: the tidy jars of nails and nuts and bolts screwed to the underside of the shelf, the tools hanging or lying upon painted outlines of themselves. He touched things reverently: a bit brace, a jack plane, the pitted and scarred vise mounted on the table's edge. Beside the vise, there was a deep-sided wooden scrap box. The last time he had come down here the sides of the box had reached nearly to his chest.

He looked down into it now and gasped.

There it was among the angular shadows: a boat. He picked it up—needed both hands. He blew at the dust and then coughed at the cloud that rose from its decks. He placed the boat on the worktable. From a hook on the wall he took a paintbrush and began to swab the decks. The brush was stiff with age, so he found an old rag, shook it clean, spat on it, and slowly washed the boat down.

It was three levels high. A tight railing of finishing nails surrounded the main deck. The ship boasted a rubber-band-operated paddle wheel at the stern and a dowel mast topped by a triangular flag.

" 'Lindy,' " he read. It was written in the best hand he could muster at ten.

Yes, he had been ten. Looking at it now, he knew exactly when he had made it. He bent down to see the boat at deck height, then he rested his arms on the worktable and his chin on his arms. He imagined himself the size of a toy captain, he imagined his mother lounging on a chair on the plywood deck playing her guitar.

"Build me a boat that will carry two."

He looked behind him suddenly, across the expanse of the shop, back down the shadowy corridor.

"Mom?" he called. He listened but all he could hear was the wind swirling around in the window wells. "Lindy?"

Nothing.

He returned his attention to the boat. Who had put it in the scrap box? He lifted it up and turned to leave, making his way back through the labyrinthine cellar, turning lights off as he went, feeling the darkness close in behind him like something chasing him and threatening to catch up to him at any moment. He found himself hurrying, until he was fairly flying. Finally he reached the stairs and looked to his right, down toward the oldest stretch of the basement. His eyes picked out a row of garden tools ranged along a wooden wall of peeling paint. He stared at the spade with its sharp point.

She never dreamed she was going to rot away in a huge empty house.

It's not possible, he told himself, and then he tore up the cellar stairs, falling in his flight and scraping his shin. He sat holding it and holding back the panic he felt inside.

He placed the boat on the shelf in Lindy's room. He was about to leave when he recalled what Sunny had said about things disappearing. He checked the bookshelf. One, two, three yearbooks: just as Sunny had said. It was her last year that was missing. Graduation year.

Getting off his knees, he was about to leave the room, when he stopped and turned and picked up the boat, cradling it in his arms. He had lost it once before; he didn't want to lose it again.

It started to rain as he made his way down the hill to Camelot. He took off his windbreaker and wrapped the boat in it. At the back door, as he returned the house key to its hook, he listened. They were downstairs in the den, Bernard and Birdie, watching television.

He made his way to his bedroom, where he placed the boat proudly on his dresser. He was shivering with cold, so he toweled himself down and changed into his pajamas. He stared at the boat, leaning close to it to count the finishing nails around the deck. There were twenty-nine.

Twenty-nine. That was how old Lindy had been when she left home. It must have been the last thing he had made her, but somehow had never had the chance to give to her. He didn't remember any kisses and hugs associated with this boat. All he remembered were tears.

THE QUEEN OF THE PUMPKIN PATCH

Dec sat at the table outside the guidance office waiting for Mr. Marlborough. Ezra sat across from him, his pointy chin resting in the cup of his hands.

"My mother's upset," he said. Dec looked at him dubiously. "She can't understand why you don't come around anymore."

Dec frowned. "And you told her I was on the verge of a nervous breakdown, I hope?"

Ezra looked surprised. "Do you really hope you'll have a nervous breakdown?"

"Idiot," said Dec.

Ezra grinned. "But seriously, why don't you come over Saturday. She'll make macaroons just for you. She likes you way more than me."

Dec smiled. "Thanks. I'd like that."

"And it might be a good idea to get away?"

"Oh, yeah," said Dec. "In fact, ask your mother if I can move in."

Then Mr. Marlborough arrived. "Ah, the brain trust,"

he said by way of a greeting. "What can I do for you, fellas?"

In a moment he had found them the 1986 edition of *The Fife and Drum* with its garish tartan cover. He owned every yearbook published in his thirty-two-year stint at Ladybank Collegiate. "I'm going to have to retire," he said, "or get me some more shelves."

Dec thanked him and was about to take the book, when something occurred to him. "Do you remember my mother?" he asked. "Lindy Polk?"

The counselor seemed to thumb through a Rolodex in his head. "Nope," he said finally. "Sadly, my memory is dominated by those students who gave me the most work." He indicated his aging face. "Every one of these wrinkles has a name."

"What about Dennis Runyon?"

Marlborough grimaced and pulled down the flesh beside his left eye. "See those crow's feet? That's Denny Runyon territory."

"That bad, eh?"

Marlborough looked thoughtful. "Yes, that bad. But you'll notice I'm pointing at what are commonly called laugh lines." He shook his head. "I remember Runyon convincing his whole class to walk clear through homeroom and out onto the roof of the tech wing."

The boys looked at each other in frank approval.

"Denny Runyon could convince a rabbit to jump into a stewing pot," said Marlborough. He laughed and then frowned again. "He convinced more than one instructor to find employment elsewhere."

Dec pictured the wired up, fast-talking water haulage man, a con artist from an early age.

"What made you think of him?" asked Marlborough. Then he stopped himself. "Oh, right! The accident. Sorry. That must have been a shock. Well, if it's any consolation, there are a lot of people who'd tell you he had it coming. Which is sad, because he was a smart cookie."

Back in the hallway, Dec and Ezra sat side by side and flipped open the yearbook. Lindy Polk was all over the place: "Hangin' with the Chick Brigade," "Home on the Range," "The Queen of the Pumpkin Patch." Here she was riding on a football player's shoulders, his helmet in her raised hands. There she was in the quad with a math book lying open on her chest, her eyes shut, "Catchin' Sum Rays." And there she was in her grad photo, her wild hair tamed for the occasion and her lipstick glistening.

Lindy Polk (Reddi Wip)
Who can forget Home Ec with BV, Geog with BV, Bookkeeping with BV. "Mamma mia, let me go!" How about that trip to Mont Tremblant . . . so many hommes so little temps. Reddi Wip is off to Saint Lawrence College for Accounting if Richy Rich doesn't make his move and whip her off to Shangri-la. Whatever, wherever . . . Go get 'em, Polkaroo!

"BV is Birdie?" asked Ezra. Dec nodded. "And Richy Rich?"

"My dad. I guess she did a co-op placement at Steeple Enterprises."

"That was how they met?"

Dec nodded. "As far as I know. He does actually go into the office sometimes. He's on the board of directors."

Ezra wiggled his eyebrows like Groucho Marx. "And what better time to drop in than when there's a fox on co-op placement." He looked at her picture and barked admiringly.

"That's my mother you're barking at," said Dec.

"Sorry."

"And, in case you'd forgotten, my dad is hardly the lecherous type." Dec looked at his mother's grad picture again. The wicked smile. "It's hard to imagine him coming on to her. He's so . . ." Dec couldn't think what.

"So *un*lecherous?"

"So . . . boring."

There was an awkward exchange of glances. Then they both turned back to the yearbook. The pages flipped past, one year in the life of a small town high school.

What was he looking for? It was like looking through *Where's Waldo?* except Dec had no idea what Waldo was. All he knew was that the yearbook was missing from Lindy's bookshelf and nothing was supposed to go missing from the House of Memory. All he could think was that somebody didn't want it lying around.

They were near the end of the book before they found anything of interest. Two boys were poised over the open hood of a car in the auto mechanics shop. They were mugging for the camera, one of them with a sledgehammer, the other holding his face in mock horror. The "victim" was Clarence Mahood.

Ezra whistled. "Pre-bald days," he said. "But you'd know that gut anywhere. Not to mention the car. It's the Duster, isn't it?"

But Dec was too busy staring at the boy with the sledgehammer. He sported a very bad shag and a wild man's grin. Dec recognized him right away.

"With a high performance V-8 and 340 horses under the hood, this Duster can take anything in town," says Clarence the hood Mahood. Wanna bet, Clare? That's Denny Runyon fixing to do some surgery!!!

"Hey!" said Ezra, who had just read the caption. "That's Runyon?"

Dec nodded.

Then it came to him. The time he had gone to Lindy in her room when she was playing the guitar. A yearbook had been open on the loveseat beside her. He tried to see the page again in his mind's eye. A dance—that was it. Immediately he began to flip back through the yearbook, his tongue between his teeth. He stopped at a two-page spread, a collage of the spring prom, "Nights in the Kasbah."

"Yes!" he said, stabbing at one of the pictures with his finger. It was Runyon all right, although it was easy to see why he hadn't noticed him earlier. He was in some kind of an Arabian getup with a fez perched on his head. He was flexing his biceps for the camera. A girl wearing harem pants, a halter top, and veil, like a genie from some corny *Arabian Nights* movie, was draped over his shoulders, her arms tight around his neck.

Lindy Polk.

THE SUPER EXCAVATOR

They had gone to the spring prom together in '86. By July, Denny Runyon had left town and Lindy was married to Bernard Steeple and pregnant with Declan. She lived for more than ten years in a house that became a prison to her with a man she grew to despise. Then she flew the coop, with only two postcards to indicate the direction of her flight. Five years later, Denny Runyon died in that same house.

"It explains one thing," said Dec.

"What's that?"

"Why they didn't want me at the inquest."

He waited for Ezra to refute what he had said with some implacable logic. But Ezra only nodded. "You're right. It would have had to come up. Probably that's why Mahood was at the inquest."

Dec looked stonily at the table. First bell had come and gone. Second bell as well. They were all alone at the table outside the guidance office and no one seemed to care. The yearbook still lay open in front of them. Dec felt numb.

Finally Ezra patted him on the arm. "The coroner obviously reached the conclusion that there was no connection between Lindy and Runyon's relationship and Runyon's death."

"How can you say that?"

Ezra shrugged. "If there was even a hint of foul play, the case would have gone to court for a proper trial. That's what an inquest is all about."

The news did little to relieve Dec of the niggling doubt he felt or of his resentment. It stuck in his craw. Why all the secrecy? Why had they treated him like a child? He felt his mother at his ear whispering to him, cajoling him.

Ezra took off his tiny, thick glasses and cleaned them on the tail of his shirt. "You know," he said, "they might have had a good reason for not telling you."

"Like what?"

"Like it would make the accident seem worse."

Dec scoffed. "The guy died. How much worse could it get?"

"Look at it from their point of view," said Ezra. "They figure, Hey, this kid is traumatized enough. If he finds out Runyon wasn't just any old stranger, maybe it's going to plunge him into despair."

Dec grinned. "*Plunge* me into despair?"

Ezra placed his specs back on his nose. "A sensitive guy like you," he said. "Who knows?"

Dec felt foolish. He *was* sensitive—too sensitive for his own good. He looked at the picture of his mother, the smile in her eyes. He looked at the boy whose neck her arms were draped around. There was no tattoo there, not yet.

Ezra closed the yearbook. "Talk to your dad, Dec," he said. "The truth shall set you free."

And that was what he planned to do. But his dad wasn't home. He was in Kingston according to Mary, Sunny's babysitter. Wouldn't be back until that night sometime. Dec wasn't about to ask Birdie. They weren't fighting exactly, but their communications had reached the pass-the-butter stage. Sometimes when their eyes met he saw a reflection of his own resentment. And sometimes he thought he saw something like fear.

Sunny's ear was still bothering her. She kept whining and wanting him to read to her. By dinner he was Sunnyed out, so, ignoring his apprehensions about the place, he grabbed his backpack and his computer and headed once more to the big house. He had a 90 percent average he planned to keep come hell or high water, and exams were just around the corner. Getting out of here had never seemed more important.

Steeple Hall loomed before him. He had lost his mother there and found her again, but not the mother he had expected. He wasn't sure if his memory was betraying him or enlightening him, but either way, he didn't think he could take much more of it.

He set up his iBook in his grandfather's study and stared at the screen, trying not to listen for a voice in every creak and groan of the wind-shifting night. His imagination wanted to wander off up the spiral stairs or drift down into the cellar. He tried not to think of the cellar at all.

He finished "Frozen Music," ending the paper with a quote by Frank Lloyd Wright: "The physician can bury his mistakes, but the architect can only advise his client to plant vines." It was a good quotation. It made him think of the fairy tale in which briars grew up around the castle where the princess lay in a dead sleep. It made him think of how the briars, sharp as razors, grew so thickly they completely consumed the castle until it was lost to view.

He closed his laptop. It was after nine. He knew he should go, but he stayed another moment. He wasn't sure why.

There was a telephone on the desk. It was a homely black article with the number PAcific 2-3039 typed on a little circle of yellowing paper in the center of the dial. He picked up the receiver. It had been disconnected a long time ago. The new phone line would service only the security system. There was no way to call out of the House of Memory. He put down the receiver and imagined a telephone that connected you to the past.

The wind was picking up. It rattled the windows in their sockets. He pushed himself free of the desk, glancing below it, glad to see the space empty. Opening the door, he stepped into the hall. He reached back to turn off the study lights and she was on him like a shot.

"Where have you been?" she demanded.

He cringed. "Leave me alone!"

"Oh, don't be such a wimp," she said. "You are so like your father sometimes." Then she took him by the hand and started dragging him upstairs.

"You're hurting me," he cried. His hand was so small, her pull so large. He felt her fingernails dig into his skin.

"Mommy," he said, pleading.

She wasn't listening. She was agitated about something, wanted to show him something. He fell on the stairs and she dragged him back up to his feet as if he were a dog on a leash. She led him to his father's childhood room and slammed the door behind them.

"There," she said triumphantly, her body pressed against the door.

"I don't want to play hiding on Daddy," whined Dec.

"Then you haven't been paying attention," she hissed. She returned to the door, listening intently as if someone was after them. When she was satisfied that no one was coming, she turned to him. "Time for a history lesson," she said.

She looked old. There were bags under her eyes and her skin looked as pale as bread dough. She was wearing raggedy jeans and a pink T-shirt with a kitten on it. Her hair was tied back in a scruffy ponytail. There was a slur to her speech as if she'd been drinking. She liked to burn the candle at both ends, she had told him once. He had wondered how you did that, where you held the thing.

She led him to a corner of the room where a magnificent construction sat. It was made of Meccano pieces. The Super Excavator.

"Look," she demanded.

The excavator stood on its own small stand. She turned on the light above it. "I want to tell you a story," she said.

"About Daddy's excavator? I know that story."

"Not all of it," she said sharply. "It required one hundred and fifteen parts to make this thing, Dec."

"I know. Daddy told me. The Master Engineer's Set. He got it for Christmas."

"One hundred and fifteen parts," she said again, as if trying to find her place in the story. "But that wasn't *all* the parts in the Master Engineer's Set. When he was done, there was a handful of stuff left in the box."

Dec was quiet now. This was new territory. His father hadn't told him about spare parts.

She knelt behind him, steadied herself with a hand on his shoulder. She reached out to turn the crank, make the bucket go up and down, up and down. Then she leaned close to whisper in his ear, so close that the smell of alcohol made him feel woozy.

"I asked myself what he did with the leftovers."

Dec didn't understand. He was mesmerized by the bucket going up, going down.

"What do you think, huh?"

Dec bit the inside of his mouth.

She laughed. "Well, I'll tell you then. He chucked them."

He reached out to try the crank himself.

"He threw them away, Dec."

She pulled his hand away from the crank. "Are you even listening to me?"

"Yes," he said, his voice barely a whisper.

"Think of it," she said. "The set was brand-new that very day, a Christmas present. And he just threw out what he couldn't use."

Then Dec felt her wrap her arms around his chest and lay her head against his back. He felt the weight of her on him. He felt her voice more than heard it, felt it resonate through his torso, her voice journeying back to him through so many years.

"You see, he doesn't really keep *everything*," she said. "Whatever doesn't fit, he gets rid of."

A FULL MOON NIGHT

He sat in the gloom of his own small room in Camelot. He sat holding himself until the darkness settled down around him—his clothes on the floor, his books on the shelves, his clutter on the desk. Far away, in the TV room, Birdie was watching a sitcom alone. He could hear the laugh track. It helped somehow.

Without turning on the light, he sat at his desk, plugged his iBook into the wall jack, and went online. He worked in a darkness diminished only by the light glowing on the screen.

It was just after ten when his father knocked quietly and poked his head in the door. Dec swiveled around in his chair, instinctively shifting to hide the screen from his father's eyes.

"Hi," said his father softly. His face was in shadows. "You wanted to see me?"

Dec recovered his composure. "Uh, yeah," he said. "Give me a minute."

There was a beat before his father nodded. "Is anything wrong?"

"I'll close up," said Dec abruptly. His voice was shaky.

"What is it, son?" asked his father, stepping into the room.

"For Christ's sake," said Dec, closing the cover of his laptop.

But not fast enough.

"What is that?" his father asked, straining to see the disappearing screen. And Dec slowly pushed the lid open again and slumped back in his chair so his father had a clear view of where Dec had been traveling.

He had scanned two images into the computer. They were both of Lindy. One was a wedding picture. She was all in white with yellow flowers woven into her red hair. Her cheeks were flushed, as if maybe she had drunk a fair bit of champagne. In the other picture, her face was in profile, her hair pulled back. She was playing her guitar, bending over it, sitting on the edge of the loveseat.

"I posted them in a missing persons cybercenter," said Dec.

"Missing persons?" His father looked at him incredulously.

"Yeah, well . . ."

His father wiped his face with his large hand. He looked around kind of numbly, then made his way in the semidark to Dec's bed, where he sat.

Dec switched on his desk lamp, logged off, and closed down the computer. "I tried to tell you," he said. "She's been on my mind lately."

"So I gather. And this is, presumably, because of Birdie and me."

Dec cleared his throat, or tried to. "That's part of it," he said. "But other stuff, too." He rubbed his eyes, pressed hard on the lids. "The dead guy, for instance," he said without looking at his father.

"Dennis Runyon."

Dec glanced up at his dad, made eye contact, nodded. "Weird, how I didn't know who he was."

His father regarded him steadily. "And what is it you think you do know?"

Dec swallowed hard but could not dislodge the lump in his throat. "They went out together. Mom and Denny."

"So? Your mother went out with a lot of boys."

"Okay," said Dec, "but as far as I know, only one of them ended up dead in our house."

Bernard stared at him, his large hands on his knees, his whole body as still as a sphinx. "What exactly is that supposed to mean, Declan?"

Dec turned back to his desk, unable to take the sphinx's gaze and unable to answer the riddle it posed him. "I don't know," he said. "That's what I really wish someone would tell me."

He glanced at his father. Bernard was looking down

at the rug. "It doesn't mean anything." Then he looked up. "They were *all* friends, son. Your mother and Birdie, Denny and Clare Mahood."

Dec folded his hands on his laptop. "Then why is everything so hush-hush?"

His father sighed. "You're making too much of things."

"*I'm* not the one making too much of things. You lie to me about not knowing who Runyon was, you stop me from going to the inquest, you even remove the yearbook with Mom and Runyon in it so that I won't see it."

"What?" He saw his father's eyes narrow. "What are you talking about?"

"Her senior yearbook. It's gone."

"I don't know anything about that," said his father. "Maybe Sunny—"

"Sunny was the one who noticed it was gone."

His father looked thoughtful. "I can't explain it," he said. "I imagine it will show up eventually. Surely that's not why you're acting this way."

"Acting what way?"

"So hot under the collar. Yes, Lindy dated Runyon. For a month or two. That was all. He got himself involved in some shady business and took off out of town with the law on his tail. End of story. What happened—him coming back, meeting you, deciding to rob the big house—that's all coincidence. Nothing but coincidence."

His voice was unruffled, a father's voice. The kind of voice he would have used to talk Dec down from a nightmare. Dec fidgeted in his seat. He could feel Lindy prodding him, moving inside him, as if his eyes were knot-holes in a fence and she wanted a peek—wanted to gauge Bernard's reaction for herself.

Dec could almost hear her whispering, "Bernard Steeple doesn't like this one bit."

"Yeah, but it is pretty weird," said Dec.

Bernard Steeple, meanwhile, held Dec in a steady gaze. Maybe he caught a glimpse of Lindy in Dec's eyes.

"I don't know what's got into you," he said. "But since you want to know, I'll tell you." He paused. "One way or another, your mother knew just about every lowlife in the county." He gave Dec a there-are-you-happy look. "When she married me, it was a big step up the ladder, one she was happy to make at first. Then, to make a long story short, it soured. These things happen." He rested his elbows on his knees. His fingers pressed together, intertwining, then com-ing apart. "You know what she was like," he said, and his voice quaked. It was the first sign of any emotion and he immediately squelched it. He got up. If he had expected a reply, he didn't wait for it. He closed the door softly behind him.

Dec found him sitting in his favorite chair in the den. Birdie's sitcom was long since over. Bernard was alone, nursing a cup of tea.

"I'm sorry," said Dec.

His father looked at him squarely. "So am I."

"I didn't mean to be stupid," said Dec. "I'm just trying to figure out about her—about Mom. About what happened."

His father reached out and touched him lightly on the chest. "I'm sorry I barked at you. You stirred up old feelings, I guess. Your mother left me, Dec. It's not something a man feels proud of. You can understand that, can't you? It's not something I want to be reminded of."

Dec sat on the edge of Birdie's chair, identical to his father's with just the side table between them for their cups of tea at night. "I can understand that," he said. "What I don't understand is why you'd hide everything from me."

His father looked at him as if seeing him differently. "No," he said. "You're not exactly a baby anymore." He pinched his nose, rubbed his eyes. Blinked. "So. What is it you want to know?"

Dec shrugged. What *did* he want to know? Where was he supposed to start? "I found this boat," he said. "I made it for Mom. It was a birthday present, I guess. But I found it in the scrap bin down in Granddad's shop. I remember all kinds of things about her, about Mom. Especially lately. But I can't figure out about this boat. Why it was there."

His father looked puzzled. "This is about a boat?"

"I know it sounds dumb," said Dec. "The thing is, there is this kind of black hole when I try to remember her leaving."

His father nodded as if he understood all too well. He took a sip of his tea. "Is that the thing I saw on your dresser?" Dec nodded. "I wondered where it came from. I never saw it before." He paused, looked away a moment. "You must have made that boat for her birthday," his father said. "She left on her birthday. You don't remember that?"

Dec shook his head very slowly.

His father looked like a man about to dive into deep water. He took a deep breath. "We had a birthday party. Her twenty-ninth. I baked a cake with twenty-nine candles on it." He looked up inquisitively, as if wanting to see if Dec remembered the cake. Dec shook his head "I remember you holding Sunny up to see it," said his father, managing a sad smile. "She would have been five or six months old."

November the first, thought Dec, remembering his mother's birthday. But why had he never given her the present? Or if he had, why had it ended up in the bin? The expression on his father's face fell a little.

"Later on, after supper, your mother decided to go out with some of her friends. I didn't want to go." He laughed mirthlessly. "Not that I was invited. I went to bed around eleven, I guess. But I stayed up reading." He smiled, a pale smile. He was inside the memory now, seeing it. "I can even tell you the title of the book," he said with a glimmer of pride in his eye. "*At the Edge of History*, it was called. By William Irwin Thompson. What do you think of that? A man's wife leaves him and years later he can remember what book he was reading on the fateful night."

Dec nodded, not wanting to breathe, just wanting his father to go on. "Anyway, around two a.m. I turned out my bedside lamp. But before I got to sleep I saw headlights on the bedroom wall. A car was coming up the hill. I got up and went to the window. You know how the master bedroom windows look out over the front entrance? Well, by then the car was in the roundabout. It was a full moon night and I could see it clear as day. A Crown Royal. Bernice Woolsey's old Crown Royal. Now there was a firetrap of a car, if I ever saw one. Anyway, Bernice was one of your mother's gang, although I could never figure it out, since she wasn't exactly the partying type. I used to think it was because she didn't drink. She was always the designated driver."

Dec looked at his father but didn't say anything, not wanting to break the spell. His father was warming to his story now, looking more alive somehow, as if he was happier when he was back in some other time, even a terrible one.

"I saw your mother get out of the car and come around toward the entrance. Then Bernice got out all of a sudden and gave her a big hug. When I thought about it later, I understood what that hug was about. But at the time, it just seemed . . . well, you know, women . . . I didn't understand that she was saying goodbye." He looked up to see if Dec understood.

"Go on," said Dec.

His father took another deep breath, dove again. "I went back to bed. But after a while I wondered where Lindy was. I gave her a few more minutes, figured maybe she'd gone to the kitchen to get a bite to eat. Then I began to wonder if she had fallen or something. Sometimes when she got back from a night on the town, she would be a little unsteady on her pins."

"Unsteady on her what?"

"Inebriated," said his father. "I got up and went downstairs. I was still on the stairs when I heard a car. I went to the front door, thinking Bernice had come back. And that's when Lindy came around from the back, from the garage. She was driving the Wildcat. I ran out onto the porch, down onto the roundabout, but she was already heading down the hill."

He paused, his eyes on that long-ago scene. "I was frantic, Dec. She knew how to drive. But she was drunk, as far as I knew. And she didn't have a license. She'd lost it—too many speeding tickets. I thought about taking off after her, but what good would that do? Besides, I couldn't leave you two alone. So I thought about calling the cops. And I was just about to do it—was already dialing the number—when I realized something and put the receiver down."

"What?"

His father looked at him. "She was in jeans and a jacket," he said.

Dec shook his head. "I don't understand."

"No, of course you don't. I haven't explained this very well. When she left to go out earlier that night, she was dressed to the nines. This tight-fitting, slinky yellow number with a slit up one leg, high heels, her hair all done up, as if maybe she and the girls were heading to Vegas or something. But when she climbed out of Bernice Woolsey's Crown Royal, she was in jeans and a jacket."

He waited, let Dec figure it out himself. "Her getaway clothes," said Dec. "So the whole thing was planned?" His father nodded, his face a muddle of expressions.

Bernard shrugged, and, despite the years that had passed, Dec could see the shadow of betrayal in his eyes. He didn't speak for a moment. Then he cleared his throat. "I stood out under that cold full moon shivering a bit. I thought about it. About the way she'd been driving. Not like a lunatic, not like a drunk. She must have sobered up since she had left the house at eight or so." He shook his head, but there was almost a look of admiration in his eyes.

"I went to her room," he said. "We still shared the master bedroom, but she had the other room—her sitting room. She hadn't taken much. Her guitar was gone. I noticed that right away. So was her backpack. I don't know what else. But it suddenly seemed pretty clear. It hadn't been an impulsive act."

Dec nodded slowly, letting it sink in. As he did, the black hole dissolved. He could see it all clearly now. He could remember the slinky yellow dress. He could remember Lindy trying to kiss him good night, all dolled up and stinking so much of perfume he had to hide his head under his pillow.

Dec stood at his window in the dark. It was well into the night now. He looked out at the ragged moonscape. He was thinking about his father's story. And he was remembering his ten-year-old self, wandering in his pajamas down the wide hallway of the big house, wandering in the dark to the upstairs hall window, the same window at which she had waited for him as Wonder Woman.

He had gone to the window to stand lookout. He had gone to the window because he wanted to be the first one to greet Lindy Polk when she came home from her holiday. That was what his father had told him, that his mother was taking a little holiday. What else could he say? Dec remembered wanting to be the one to see her coming up the hill. He wanted to be the one who raced down the stairs to the door and flung it open for her, took her backpack and her guitar and welcomed her home. He wanted to give her the present he had made for her. He squeezed his eyes shut, but a tear burrowed its way out, escaping the web of his eyelashes to slide down his cheek. He remembered being frightened. Frightened that his mother might not find her way back to the house even if she wanted to. Because it was so very, very dark.

A LATE NIGHT CALL

The call came after eleven. Dec was already in bed when Birdie appeared at his door with the portable phone in hand. She frowned as she handed it to him. He returned her frown and waited with the receiver pressed to his chest until she retreated, closing the door behind her.

"Hello?"

"Guess who."

He went cold all over. It was her. Lindy. He sat up, collecting what was left of his tattered nerves, regaining his wits.

"Are you there, Dec?"

He couldn't believe his mistake. "Vivien?"

"You thought it was someone else, didn't you?"

"No," he lied. "I'm just slow."

"Sorry to be calling so late. Is your mother really mad?"

He was going to correct her, but it was too late to start explaining things. "No, it's cool," he said.

"And I'm sorry about the whole guess-who routine. God, that is so lame."

Dec smiled. It was a crazy lady, all right, but good crazy. "Did you just phone to apologize?"

"Oh, what a goof," she said. "I mean *me*, not you. I'm . . . No, I won't say it."

His grin widened. He hoped she could feel it when he spoke. "We don't take any classes together," he said, "so I'm guessing this isn't about homework."

"Right. You're absolutely right. This is not about homework. I was talking to Ezra the other day about his scholarship."

Dec laid his head back on his pillow. "Uh-huh."

"It's brilliant," she said. "I mean, for him. But, well, I saw you later that day in study hall and I thought how hard it was going to be for you when he's gone."

Dec was taken aback. Was he that transparent? Or was Vivien just that tuned in? "That must have been when I was spray-painting the big sign on the wall, 'Don't go, Ezra!' "

"Well, sorta," she said, laughing. "I remember how hard it was leaving my friends when I moved here. There was this one girl, Pixilene. We were like tight, really tight. And I got to this place where I couldn't breathe thinking about her not being around. You know?"

"Yeah. I think I do."

"And that's why I'm calling," said Vivien. "Well, sort of. Pixilene and me—we're *still* tight. I mean she's out in Saskatoon but we're, you know, in touch. She's probably even going to come out this summer, which is totally cool. I hope you'll meet her."

Dec settled his head into his pillow. "Is this a setup for a blind date?"

"No way!"

He smiled. "I think I know what you mean," he said. "Life goes on."

"Exactly. And this is good practice."

"For what?"

"Life. I don't know about you, but I plan on seeing a lot of the world, and so it might end up that all my friends are somewhere else. You know what I mean?"

"I think I do."

There was a pause of about twenty years. Then Dec said, "Thanks for calling. I was feeling down."

"Good," she said. "I mean *bad*." Then she laughed and her voice seemed to relax a bit. He hadn't really noticed how coiled up she had sounded until then. "That isn't the only reason I called. I was watching you—like I said—and I . . . well, I wrote this poem. Don't worry, I'm not going to read it to you."

"Thank God," he said, laughing.

"You looked so alone, so kind of . . . deserted? Anyway, I wrote this poem. And I liked it a lot. I *always* like a new poem a lot. You need to, if it's going to, you know, not *die*. You need to adore it into existence. Then later you can tear it to shreds or fix it or whatever. So as I was saying, I really liked this poem and I thought I might send it to you."

"Cool. I'll look forward to it."

"You don't have to," she said. "You can just chuck it if you like. I won't mind. You may *hate* it."

"Why?"

"I don't know. You may think it sucks. I almost put it in the mailbox, and then I went, No way!"

"So, let me get this straight . . . you didn't send it."

"No, but I still might." She laughed nervously. "I just don't want you to think I'm this freak who's like stalking you."

Just then there was a knock on his door. He raised his head enough to see Birdie in her bathrobe pointing at her watch.

"I'm getting dirty looks," he said. Birdie made a face but backed out of the room. He waited until she was good and gone. "I'll see you tomorrow," he said into the phone.

"Cool," she said, as if it wasn't just school. As if tomorrow was this idea they both shared.

A TURN OF THE TIDE

Ezra picked up Dec at four on Saturday. He drove a decrepit Toyota Tercel he called Ran. *Ran* was the name of a Japanese movie by Akira Kurosawa, but as Ezra liked to say, it was also the past tense of *run*. The Tercel was a washed-out red with rust like an old lady's liver spots on all its extremities. He pulled in between the silver Rendezvous and the jet-black Beetle, and Dec watched Bernard and Birdie grimace at the sight of it.

"Are you sure you can afford the time with exams so near?" his father asked.

"Give the kid a break," said Birdie. But the look in her eyes suggested that she might be the one who needed a break.

On the journey into town, Dec recounted his father's story, recalling his itemized memory of the event.

"Well, that clears up a whole bunch of things," said Ezra.

"Maybe," said Dec. "If you believe it."

Ezra glanced at him inquisitively.

"Well, look at the facts," said Dec. "Isn't that what you always tell me? This book he was reading for instance, *At the Edge of History*. He didn't say whether it was hardcover or paperback, whether he borrowed it from the library or bought it. I mean, how am I supposed to trust a guy who can't remember important details like that, huh?"

Ezra's smile was wry. "I get your point," he said. "He's got a fanatically good memory. But then he's into history, right?"

"Lost in it," said Dec.

"The devil's in the detail," said Ezra with a shrug. "Tell me more about this full moon night."

They arrived at Ezra's place to a clamorous reception from his dog, Schmootz, kisses and hugs from Mrs. Harlow, and a riddle from Mr. Harlow.

"Brothers and sisters have I none,
But that man's father is my father's son."

"Easy," said Ezra. "It's you."

"My son, such a smart cookie," said Mr. Harlow, beaming.

Ezra's room was a fabulous mess. Dec made his way to a blue chair shaped like an egg on a silver swivel. It was sixties kitsch, something Ezra had rescued from the dump. You didn't sit on it, you sat *in* it, enveloped in a blue shell. Ezra went immediately to his desk and switched on the computer, while Dec pushed himself around. The egg wobbled precariously.

Ezra drummed his fingers on his desk, waiting for a connection. "Something is bugging me," he said.

"Something is always bugging you," said Dec from the shadows of the blue egg. "It's congenital."

Ezra tapped at his keyboard. "When in doubt, ask Jeeves," he said.

"Ask him what?"

But Ezra's attention was absorbed by what he was doing. Dec reached down from the egg and lifted a book that lay open on the floor. There was a half-finished bag of corn chips underneath. He picked it up, shook a few into his hand, tasted one. Antique.

"Interesting," said Ezra. He punched Print. The printer buzzed and beeped and, a moment later, spat out a single sheet. Ezra looked it over and then handed it to Dec.

Dec wasn't sure what he was looking at. " 'Web Magician Wizard's Realm'? Is this an online game?"

"It's a full moon calculator," said Ezra. "You enter the year and month, and the calculator tells you the full moon for any date between 1600 and 2199. Like for instance, November 1997."

Dec looked down at the printout. The moon was full November fourteenth. "At 14:13," he said. "That's like two in the afternoon."

Ezra nodded slowly but made no comment.

"And that would mean . . ." said Dec. But he wasn't sure what it meant. Except that November first was almost two weeks earlier. He looked at Ezra again. "There wouldn't have been any moon at all the night Lindy left."

Ezra returned his gaze with a sober expression Dec didn't entirely like. He looked at the printout again. "It would have been pitch-black the night of her party," he said. He looked at his friend. Behind him, the computer went to a screen saver of flying toasters.

"Dec," said Ezra quietly. "You knew it yourself. You said you stood at the hallway window waiting for your mother to come home, worrying about how dark it was."

Dec was too stunned to nod.

Ezra shrugged. "It just seemed odd to me," he said. He scratched his head, averting his eyes. And in the gesture, Dec was suddenly struck by the enormity of what Ezra was telling him. His father's elaborately detailed story wasn't true. It was a lie.

He didn't go home that night. He needed time to think. When he phoned Camelot, he was glad it was Birdie who answered.

"Ezra's helping me with my physics," he said.

"Tell me another one," she said.

"Actually, we scored some crack and we're just about to do up."

"That's more like it," said Birdie. "You want to talk to your dad?"

Dec could hear the TV, some show they were watching from their side-by-side matching chairs. It seemed as far away as the moon.

"No," he said. "No, I don't."

Dec sat with a popcorn bowl in his lap, picking through the kernels for edible remnants. The TV was on, *Saturday Night Live*. Lots of laughs, but only from the studio audience. Ezra sat beside Dec, stretched out, his feet up on the coffee table.

"There's probably a totally rational explanation," he said.

"That's what I was thinking," said Dec. "Like he murdered her and buried her in the basement."

Ezra groaned. "Not this again."

"Well, what am I supposed to think?" Dec stared at the tube, daring the actors to make him laugh. "He's a fake. Everything he does is fake. He fights fake wars. He tells fake stories. Maybe he's not even my real father."

Ezra picked up the remote and pressed Mute. The laughter stopped. "Want to run that by me again?" he said.

Dec gave up on the popcorn. "I was thinking about Denny Runyon," he said. "About what happened when he dropped me off that day."

"The Look," said Ezra.

"Right," said Dec. "Maybe what it meant was, 'Hey, kid, you are looking at your daddy.'"

Ezra peered at Dec. "Maybe you *are* on crack."

Dec shoved him away. "Think about it. Runyon and my

mom were together at the spring prom. My birthday's in March."

"Yeah, which means that you were conceived in July. We've done the math. Runyon was out of town by then."

"According to *who*?"

"Your father," said Ezra.

"I rest my case."

Ezra leaned in very close. "I don't want to rain on your paranoid parade, Dec, but you really look like Bernard Steeple."

"Thanks a million."

Ezra leaned close again. "It wasn't an insult."

"Mr. Rogers, the Second."

"The new improved version. Better sneakers."

Dec clammed up. There was no real question in his mind that Bernard was his father. That was why the whole thing was so infuriating. He thought of his father's long face, his sincere face. And that was it! That sincere face had lied to him. Outright.

Dec reached for the remote and punched the mute button again. The show burst back into life. More laughs. Mindless. Perfect.

Ezra fell asleep curled up on the couch. Dec turned off the tube, threw a blanket over his friend, and headed upstairs to Ezra's room. Mrs. Harlow had changed the sheets for him. He stripped down to his boxers and crawled into the coolness, snuggled under the comforter. He was exhausted. Way too tired to sleep. He kept going over his father's story, again and again, drifting through the no-man's-land between wakefulness and sleep so gradually that he didn't notice when he crossed the border.

His father is still talking, still telling his story, but suddenly the account of Lindy's last night at the big house has a laugh track. Some of the biggest laughs come from Lindy herself. And when that doesn't get enough attention, she blows on her toy whistle, which drowns out everything that Bernard is trying to say. Dec wishes she would stop. It is impossible to think straight with her around.

Suddenly his father loses his patience and turns on her. "You're driving me around the bend," he says.

"That would make for a change," says Lindy. "Around the bend is farther than we've been in years."

More laughter.

A comedy sketch, except that it isn't funny.

"Please, Mom," Dec cries, grabbing at her arm, but she is made of dream material and he can't hold her.

"I'm going crazy," says Bernard, covering his ears.

"That makes two of us," says Lindy. Then she blows her whistle—loud—and marches around the room. Bernard grabs for her but he can't hold her either.

"Give that thing to me, or else!" he shouts.

"Or else what?" she shouts back.

The shout woke him. He looked around and for a moment had no idea where he was. Then he saw the shadowy shape of Ezra's egg.

Just a dream, he told himself as he gathered the comforter back off the floor. Was it a dream? Had there been a scene like that, so horrible he had repressed it? You heard stories about such things. Maybe it had happened like that. Maybe his father had snapped. Was that what he was covering up?

Dec tried to summon up such a memory, but it wasn't there. You had to go with what you knew—what you knew in your heart. You had to distinguish between what was real and what was imaginary, separate the data from the interpretation. So what did he know?

He lay there quietly, calmly, going over it all again, turning over every stone, trying to find the missing piece of the puzzle. And then he dreamed again.

A small house in a dark forest. He knocks on the door. It opens on the smiling face of Denny Runyon. There is an arrogance behind his smile that Dec hasn't noticed before.

"You know who I am," says Runyon. "Think back, amigo. Back. Remember?"

THE LIE OF THE ROOM

In the old days the Steeples had kept a boat or two down on the river. There were photographs in the drawing room of ancient relatives sailing around dressed in formal attire, a lady in a rowboat with a parasol, someone dressed up like a *coureur de bois* kneeling in a birchbark canoe. You could sail all the way to Ladybank in those days.

Now the river was not so high and Bernard had let the dock slip into decay. There was more of it below the waterline than above it. Dec tossed a stone and watched it sink until it lay on the slimy surface of the old dock. He looked at his watch. Four o'clock.

It had rained again Sunday night. All around him was the sound of dripping leaves. He picked up another stone. He hurled it, and when it sank he watched the ripples spread out until they came back to him in ever-diminishing size, so that what finally reached him was little more than the memory of a splash.

His father had driven Sunny to her ear specialist's appointment in Ottawa. Enticements were needed to get her to go: supper at a fast-food place at the very least, perhaps a trip to Mrs. Tiggy-Winkle's Toy Store. Monday was Birdie's day off and she had gone with them. Dec had taken the bus home. He had the place all to himself. But not for long. Through the thick bush along the riverbank, he heard the sound of someone approaching on the old road. He climbed to his feet, dusting the dirt from his hands. Ezra appeared.

"Come on," said Dec, and Ezra followed without a word. They scrambled up the hill, crossed the lawn, and entered the big house, where they sat on the pew in the vestibule to take off their sopping sneakers.

At the landing they turned toward Dec's old room. He closed the door behind them and went directly to his desk, opened the drawer, and took out the postcards from his mother. He handed them to Ezra.

"Is this all there is?"

Dec shrugged. "That's all she wrote."

Ezra examined the postcards minutely. "Not exactly chosen for their sentimental value," he said, looking at the pictures. He glanced at Dec.

"Keep looking."

Ezra returned his attention to the cards. "They look like maybe they got dropped in a puddle or something," he said at last. He compared the cards. "Two puddles. One in Winnipeg and one in Edmonton."

"You're getting warm," said Dec drily.

The message on each card was legible and so was the address, but the cards were both smeared in the upper-right-hand corner, where the postmarks were. Ezra looked up at Dec again. "They could have been mailed anywhere."

"Bingo," said Dec, but there was no elation in his voice. He took the cards from Ezra and stared at them. "Right here in Ladybank, for instance."

Ezra adjusted his glasses. "Lead on," he said. They left the room and headed down the corridor to his father's childhood room. Cowboys on the bedspread, cowboys on the curtains, model airplanes in the air. Battleships and destroyers, corvettes and minesweepers patrolling the shelves nearby. A book open on the bedside table: *Tom Swift and his Ultrasonic Cycloplane*. And standing in the corner, the Super Excavator. It looked menacing to Dec now, as if it might spring to life of its own accord. And who knew what it might dig up.

From under the cowboy-covered bed, Dec wheeled out a wooden drawer. He took out a fat scrapbook, laid it on the carpet, and, kneeling, opened it.

Ezra knelt beside him. "What's this?" he asked.

"When my father was little, he and his folks traveled across the country by train." Dec turned the pages of the scrapbook. Little Bernard had kept everything: the kiddy menus from the dining car, the sightseeing pamphlets, snapshots with crinkly edges, and postcards. All kinds of postcards. Some of the postcards were pasted in. But there was a small collection of them loose in the back. There were lots of cards, scenic sites: Halifax, Moncton, Quebec City, Montreal, Toronto, Winnipeg, Regina, Edmonton . . .

Dec watched Ezra shuffle through the cards, once, then again. Waited to see the exact moment when the truth dawned on him. "These are the same vintage as your mother's postcards."

Dec nodded. He closed the book and carefully replaced it in the drawer.

"Weird," said Ezra, sticking his hands in his back pockets.

"One more stop," said Dec.

They went to Lindy's room. He took one of the three remaining yearbooks and opened it to the front where Lindy had signed her name and scribbled out her address.

Ezra didn't need to be told what he was looking at. He shook his head. "The writing's nothing like on the postcards," he said.

"Oh, a little bit," said Dec. "Enough to fool a ten-year-old."

They walked together down the earthen stairs back to the dock. Dec stopped.

"This is where I was building the raft that time when Lindy and I saw the deer." He pointed to where the old road started into the woods. "Except it wasn't a deer."

"What do you mean?"

"It was a man."

Ezra stared at him. "A man dressed as a deer? Two men perhaps?"

Dec smiled, but it didn't last. "I'm not sure what it

was—it was just a glimpse. What I remember most is how hard Lindy tried to convince me it was a deer. But when I try to remember it, I don't see any antlers."

Ezra cocked an eyebrow. "Runyon?" Dec nodded. Then Ezra stared back toward the woods, as if waiting for the creature—man or beast—to appear again. "Are you *sure?*"

Dec shook his head. "Do I look like I'm sure? But he was around. That much I know."

Ezra didn't look so certain.

"I finally realized what the look on his face was when he dropped me off that day. It wasn't that he was trying to tell me something. That's where I went wrong. His smile made a big impression on me because I had seen it before. The time I took Sunny to the creek to look at the tadpoles. I saw Lindy come down the hill from the big house and throw out her thumb to hitch a ride. When the guy stopped, he reached over to open the passenger door. He was facing me although he didn't see me. He was smiling at her. *That's* where I saw that smile before."

They walked in silence along the old rutted road toward Ezra's car. The undergrowth pressed in on them; they had to walk in single file. More than once Ezra looked back. "I feel like we're being followed," he whispered to Dec.

Dec stopped and looked back along the muddy path. They waited, heard nothing. "Maybe I just feel like somebody *should* be following us," said Ezra.

They moved on. There were puddles to ford and fallen trees to clamber over. Every now and then there were glimpses of the river on their left. Every now and then there were shrieks and skitterings in the dense bush to their right where the hill climbed steeply to the grounds of the Hall.

Ezra had backed Ran down over the culvert, then parked it out of view of County Road 10 behind a wall of greenery. It had been Dec's idea. He wasn't certain when his folks would get home, and he didn't want the car sitting in the driveway and the two boys not around.

Ezra climbed behind the wheel, closed his door, and rolled down the window. He gazed at Dec's face as if he was inspecting it for cracks.

"At least there's one good thing," he said. "Runyon must have already known about this back road. So you're off the hook there."

"I guess I should feel relieved," said Dec.

Ezra looked ahead, his hands curling and uncurling on the wheel. He looked up at Dec again. "You want to come home with me?"

Dec kicked at a hardened clump of earth with the muddy toe of his shoe. "No," he said. "I can't run away from this."

Neither of them said anything for a long moment. Then Ezra put his key in the ignition. "Are you scared?"

Dec thought for a moment and nodded. "But I think what scares me most is that he might lie to me again. Every time I uncover a little bit more, he feeds me just enough story to fit the facts. I want to get to the end if it."

Ezra nodded. "There's another option," he said. "Don't say anything."

"You mean forget it?"

Ezra shrugged. "Maybe the truth is overrated?" he said. Dec snorted.

"No, seriously," said Ezra. "Your father treats you right. Before this happened, your biggest complaint about him was that he was uninspiring. That's not a capital offense."

"Yeah, but what if there *was* a capital offense? That's what it looks like."

"I know what it *looks* like, but—and don't get me wrong here—your mother sounds like a complete fruitcake."

Dec bit his lip. "You don't need to tell me."

"Maybe the past is better left where it is. You're going to blow this pop stand soon enough. Do you need to take him down? Is that what this is about?"

Dec thought about it, then slowly shook his head. "It's weird what you forget. She was so much fun. I guess that's what I wanted to remember." He pounded lightly on the door with both his fists. "The thing is, now that I know this much, I can't *not* know the rest."

Ezra nodded. "Toss me a pound," he said, and their fists bumped together. Then Ezra rolled up the window. He turned on the ignition. He sat far back in his seat, like a race-car driver, his arms locked at the elbows, revving the motor a couple of times. Dec ran ahead, ducking under the low boughs until he came to the road. It was clear both ways. He waved the okay signal to Ezra, who put his foot down on the gas and then came slipping and sliding through the wall of green, fishtailing in the mud.

He almost made it.

HOME TO ROOST

Dec was in his room when the family arrived back at Camelot. He crossed the hall to the master bedroom and from the window watched his father carry Sunny, asleep on his shoulder, into the house, while Birdie collected shopping bags from the hatch of the Rendezvous. She noticed him at the window and waved, but she raised her eyebrows in a way that made him nervous. He was back at his desk when his father poked his head in at the door a few minutes later. With books all around him, it looked like he was hard at it.

"How goes the battle?" said his father.

Dec looked at the array of work before him. "I don't know," he said. "I think it's Homework three, Dec no score."

His father smiled. "Know the feeling." He looked weary and a little worried.

"Is Sunny okay?"

"She may need a hearing aid," his father said. "They're going to do some more tests." He paused. "How about you, Dec? Are you okay?"

Dec shifted in his seat. "No," he said.

176

His father stepped into the room and closed the door behind him. Dec swiveled in his chair to face him. His father leaned against the wall. He cleared his throat.

"Just as we were coming through Cupar we passed a tow truck," said his father. "It looked like he was hauling your friend's Toyota."

"Right," said Dec. "Ezra was over."

His father waited, but Dec said no more. "There was quite a mess out on the highway," said his father, "over by the old road. Looked like someone went in the ditch." Dec nodded. "I got out to look. There were car tracks right down into the bush." Dec nodded again. Maybe he wouldn't have to say much of anything. Maybe his father would just keep following the tracks all the way back to the House of Memory.

His father crossed his arms on his chest. "You want to tell me what's going on?"

Dec looked down at his desk. Where to start?

"There was no full moon the night Mom left."

His father looked perplexed. "Excuse me?"

"The night Mom left," said Dec, raising his voice. Then, remembering his little sister sleeping down the hall, he lowered it again. "I don't understand why you would lie to me about that. Then there's the postcards and—"

"Whoa," said his father. "You're losing me."

But Dec couldn't hold on anymore. "Talk to me," he said.

His father shoved his hands in his pockets. He looked

old suddenly, defeated. He gestured with his head toward the door. "Not here," he said. "I don't want to wake up Sunny."

Birdie passed them in the front hall. She was holding a cup of tea. "Cheers," she said. Neither of them responded. They clumped down to the rec room.

"Sit," said Bernard, pointing to his favorite armchair.

"I'm not a dog," said Dec.

"Please," said his father wearily. "Have a seat."

So here they were again. And Dec wondered if this was how it would be from now on, the two of them convening in the rec room to try to hammer out a past they could both live with.

"There *was* a full moon, Dec," he said. And before Dec could raise his voice in complaint, he held up his hand. "Please, listen. I can explain. There was a full moon. But it wasn't really Lindy's birthday."

Dec groaned.

"It's true. She didn't want a party on November first," his father continued. "She didn't want to be turning twenty-nine. She said, 'Twenty-nine just means you're in your thirtieth year.' And she couldn't bear the thought that she was turning thirty. That her life was . . . well, the way it was."

Bernard cracked his knuckles. "So I abided by her wishes," he said without looking up. "Her real birthday on November first came and went without a word."

"So what about the cake and the candles and the night with the girls?"

"That was a couple of weeks later, November sixteenth, to be precise."

Dec's eyes opened wide. "That's Birdie's birthday."

"Right. Birdie's birthday. It was Birdie who talked your mother into having a shared birthday celebration."

November sixteenth, thought Dec. Two days after the full moon. "Is that really what happened?"

"Go ask Birdie."

Dec was going to, but not right now. It wasn't just the moon that was out of whack.

"You know how Lindy could be, Declan. She had a very mobile mind." His father managed a watery smile. "Here it is, two weeks later, and suddenly she wants a family party as well, a cake—the whole nine yards. Just like I said."

Dec leaned back stiffly in the armchair. He didn't know whether to feel relieved or cheated. Meanwhile, his father seemed lost in thought. "I've been thinking about that boat you made. Your mom always used to prompt you about special events: birthdays, Mother's Day, Saint Patrick's Day—anything and everything. Do you remember?" Dec guessed maybe he did.

"She would count down the days on the calendar, tease you about making her something. She'd hint at what she wanted. 'Boy oh boy, I sure could do with a new ashtray,' she'd say. Things like that. You were always game." His smile broadened, then it faded. "But after the baby, Lindy kind of lost interest. The doctor said she was suffering from severe postpartum depression. I thought there was probably more to it than that, but I tried to tread lightly. Her birthday came and went without fanfare.

"Then, out of the blue, two weeks later, kaboom! There would have been no time for you to make her anything. And you were so proud of the things you made her. You were so industrious. Still are." He paused and smiled, but Dec wasn't in the market for compliments. "I guess you must have made that boat later," his father said. "The day after, perhaps? Maybe you were hoping to surprise her when she got back. You didn't know she wasn't coming back."

How could some memories be so elusive? How come there were memories you could unwrap and see every facet—every moment—while others remained hidden?

"Why didn't you tell me this the other day?"

His father raised his hands in defeat. "About the moon? It didn't occur to me. I didn't realize it was a test."

Dec folded his arms and squeezed tight. He wasn't sure what to say.

"Dec, give me a break here. It was awful when she left. I'm sure I wasn't very attentive to your needs. There was a lot of stomping around, a lot of teary bedtimes." His father leaned toward him, his hands on his knees. "Somehow we all got through it."

Dec swallowed the lump in his throat. "There's something else."

"The postcards?"

"The postcards."

His father stared at him with a look that seemed equal

parts astonishment and admiration. "I sent those cards. But I get the feeling you already know that."

"Why?"

"Isn't it obvious?"

Dec felt a twinge of frustration. "If it was obvious, I wouldn't be asking."

His father sighed. "At first, when she left, I told you she was taking a break. A little holiday. I had to. I didn't know what else to do. I think I half believed it myself. Wanted to anyway. I was hoping if she had a bit of time to herself, she'd come back. Then when the weeks passed without so much as a word, and you were so despondent, I felt I had to do something."

His father looked wistful. "It was stupid, I guess. But it seemed to help. I felt guilty about it, but I didn't want you to think that she could have just gone like that without a word."

An uneasy silence settled between them. Dec wagged his head back and forth, back and forth. It was all so easy. His father had an answer for everything. And when those answers turned out to be false, there was a whole new set, all freshly painted to look just like the truth.

His father glanced at his watch and Dec felt a surge of anger, as if all of what he had been saying was some kind of teenage blather to be waited out. And Dec was just about to call him on it when he realized he had never seen this watch before.

"That's not the watch you broke," he said.

His father followed his gaze and then held the watch up for Dec's inspection. "No, it's my father's old Waltham," he said. "It disappeared years ago and then it suddenly turned up. I had a new strap put on it, but otherwise it works like a charm."

Dec stared at the watch. It was gold and square-shaped, with a decorative leaf pattern carved into the shoulders. The face was plain—everything about it was plain—but for the scratches in the glass.

"What do you mean, it just turned up?" His voice was snappish, as if the watch was yet another lie. But his father didn't seem to notice; in fact he was gazing at the watch fondly.

"It turned up in Runyon's loot, although I have no idea where he found it. God, I had looked everywhere for this beauty." He was shaking his head with wonder. "See the greenish tinge in the abrasions?" Dec leaned closer. He nodded. "That's residue from a smoke canister that exploded in my father's face. He wore this watch into battle on D-Day. There were these smoke canisters on the carrier they used for signaling advances to the troops. One of them burst open and my dad was in the line of fire." He looked up at Dec, his eyes eager. "My father landed on Juno Beach completely green from head to foot," he said. "Can you imagine that?"

Dec peered at his father. It was as if their entire conversation was forgotten now that he was safely back in the past. None of what I'm saying makes any difference to him, thought Dec. This old watch matters more to him than I do. His father was unstrapping it now, handing it to him for closer inspection, and Dec felt the anger boil up in him. He felt an impulse to take the watch from his father and fling it across the room, smash it.

But suddenly time stopped.

He saw the watch in his father's fist, saw it glinting gold, and remembered where he had seen it before. In a dead man's clawlike grasp.

"What is it?" his father asked.

Dec took the watch, shaking his head. "Nothing," he said, handing it back immediately, not wanting to hold it.

His father strapped it back on his wrist. "It's not valuable—well, not to anyone but me, I guess." He sighed. "I once accused Lindy of stealing it just to make me angry. She knew how much I loved this thing. She insisted I had just lost it."

Dec went cold all over. He stared at his father, trying to sort the man out, and trying to sort out thoughts that were racing every which way.

"That woman," said his father. "I swear, she could drive a man to desperate lengths." He looked across the shadowy room. They had turned on only the nearest lamp. His father seemed to be trying to make out things outside of their little circle of light. "It's funny," he said. "You asked me if I ever think about her. I do, now and then. I wonder if she made it to wherever she was heading." He paused, looked down. There was a spot of gray paint on his trousers. He rubbed at it. "The big house is the only place she's still alive for me anymore. Sometimes I actually think I hear her, laughing in another room or playing her guitar."

Dec glanced up. "Really?"

His father had an amused look on his face. "She had this fool whistle."

"I know!" said Dec, a little shocked. "I've heard it. Or, I mean, I thought I did. She'd just blow it in your face." For a moment the boy and the man stared at each other in astonishment.

"You want to know something?" said his father. He was staring so hard at Dec it was almost frightening. "After she left—I mean, after I knew she wasn't coming back—I tried to find her."

Dec sat up straighter in his chair. It was as if, without ever knowing it, this was what he had wanted to hear.

"You went after her?"

His father shook his head. "I hired a private investigator."

Dec stared at his father in disbelief. "A private eye?"

"Yep."

It seemed so unreal and yet he knew, looking into his father's eyes, that this, at least, was true. And whatever else he thought, he loved his father for it. For at least trying.

"But he didn't have any luck," said Dec hesitantly.

His father's eyes grew large. "Oh, he found her, all right," he said. "It took him a few months. I guess it would have been early September. She was down in Hamilton."

He paused and his voice was hesitant when he continued. "Runyon was there."

Dec held his breath. "With her?"

His father nodded. "They were living together." He seemed to have trouble saying the words. "I'm not sure why I'm telling you this."

"Because I want to know," said Dec. He had not realized how thirsty he was to know something—to know anything.

"It's a closed book, really," said his father, his face falling.

"Tell me!" Dec demanded. It came out as a shout. "What happened?"

His father scratched his brow. "I made a fool of myself." He managed a mirthless little laugh. "Don't know what I was thinking. I just wanted her back. Told her I'd change."

"You saw her?"

"I went down there, down to Hamilton, to this squalid little apartment they were shacking up in. I waited until Runyon was out. I pleaded with her. Told her we'd travel, see the world. Anything she wanted." He looked squarely at Dec. There was a tear in his eye. "After everything," he said, his voice ragged and small. "Almost a whole year later—after everything she had done, I was still nuts about her."

Dec reached out to touch his father, but his hand never made it. There was a loud crash behind them. They both spun around. Birdie was standing in the doorway to the rec room, her teacup shattered on the linoleum.

BIRDIE SINGS

The night was full of wind, and the trees around Steeple Hall seemed intent upon trapping it all. They leaned and lunged. Their thick arms creaked with the weight and wallop of the air.

Dec bent his head and wrapped his arms tightly around his sleeping bag. It was June, but it felt like winter up here. He imagined the dark hulk of the House of Memory as a freighter tossed on a high sea. He imagined how far off course she was being blown tonight. His teeth chattering, he sped up his pace, buffeted every step of the way. As cold as it was, it was better than the storm he had left behind at Camelot.

He had no idea how long Birdie had been standing at the door to the rec room. "September?" she said, her voice thin and disbelieving. "September?" She walked toward them in her stocking feet through the shattered crockery.

Dec had jumped to his feet. "Birdie, be careful," he said. But she paid no attention.

"September," she said again, as if the name of the month itself was the concept she couldn't quite grasp.

By now Bernard was going to her, but she held up her hand and backed away. Backed away until her back was against the wall.

"Honey," said Bernard. "It was the last—" But she cut him off.

"We started building this house in September."

"I know," said Bernard.

"Our house."

"It was foolish—"

"Foolish?" Her voice was tremulous. "Foolish doesn't even start . . . It was *wrong*, Bernard. Just plain *wrong*." She smacked the wall with the flat of her hand.

"Birdie, please," said Bernard. "Let me try to explain."

"No!" she shouted. "No, no, no!"

Which was when Sunny woke up, howling.

And Dec slipped away.

He stood in the cool silence of the House of Memory. It seemed too silent. He trained his flashlight on the grandfather clock. It had stopped. His father must have forgotten to wind it.

Dec closed the door of the vestibule behind him, blocking out the wind. He listened, not sure what he expected to hear. But there was nothing. She wasn't here anymore. Her absence filled the house again, the way it had when she first left.

He made his way to his childhood room. He was so tired. Dead tired. He had made a grab at the truth and it had morphed in his hands, turning into something more slippery and strange than he could have imagined. He felt empty now. He just wanted to sleep.

The sound of a car's engine woke him. It was revving high, fighting the overgrowth on the steep driveway. As Dec struggled up from the depths of sleep, he thought it was the Wildcat—his mother returning at long last. He saw lights pass across the curtains. The car stopped in the roundabout and the lights went out. He listened. Minutes passed until he wondered if he had seen or heard anything at all.

He rubbed the sleep out of his eyes and checked the illuminated hands of his watch. It was after midnight. Finally he heard the distinctive thud of a car door. Then footsteps on gravel, on stone, on wood. He heard the front door open and close, then nothing. Thick carpet sucked up the progress of whoever was here. Though he listened with every fiber of his body, all he could hear was the creaking of the old mansion riding out the storm.

Please, God, he begged. Don't let it be her.

The door of his room opened. A woman appeared silhouetted in the entranceway.

"It's only me," she said.

"Birdie?"

"Did I wake you? Stupid question."

Her voice was flat, lifeless. Dec shinnied up to a sitting position.

"What do you want?"

"I'm not sure," she said.

Dec saw her shoulders shake. Slowly he unzipped his sleeping bag and climbed out. He stood on the rag rug some ancestor had made. He wasn't sure what to do.

"Are you all right?"

"No," she said, crossing her arms.

"What happened?"

"You want to know what happened? I'll tell you. I'm a cow, Declan. That's what happened. I'm a stupid, jealous, lying cow."

Dec switched on the flying saucer lamp on his desk. They both stood there blinking.

"You shouldn't blame yourself," he said. "It must have been a shock."

"I'm not talking about your father's confession!" she said. Her face looked ravaged, her eyes desolate. "Dec, I've done a terrible thing."

He approached her slowly, took her arm, and led her into the room. She came timidly, sniffing and searching in her pockets for a tissue. She was wearing one of his father's cardigans. Mrs. Rogers. He pulled out the chair from his desk and sat her down. Her face looked ghastly in the mica-tinted light. She shivered. He found a blanket and wrapped it clumsily around her shoulders.

"Thank you," she said, barely audible.

"You want to tell me about it?"

"You're not going to like it."

Dec pulled over a small yellow chair from the Lego table and sat at her feet. "Probably not," he said. "But I don't know how much worse things can get."

Her eyes told him a lot. And with his own eyes he said I'm ready.

"I didn't mean to be spying on you and your dad," she said. "I came downstairs to see if you wanted a cup of tea. I was glad you were talking. There's been so much *not* talking lately." She blew her nose and then jumbled up the wet tissue in her hand.

He couldn't remember if he had ever seen her so un-put-together. She bit her lip. She wiped her bloodshot eyes. Then she dug something out of the cardigan pocket. It was a compact disc. She handed it to him.

"It's from Lindy," she said.

Dec didn't understand. Lindy had sent him a CD? Then he looked at the picture on the cover. It *was* Lindy. He held it near the lamp. Lindy's face almost filled the cover. It might have been the greenish-yellow light, but she looked older, thinner in the cheek. Her eyes seemed paler than he recalled, but there was wind and sunlight in her hair and she was smiling at something she saw in the sky.

"It arrived in late November."

"Last *fall*?"

"From California."

He read the title. "*What I Can.*"

Dec flipped over the CD. There was another picture. Lindy standing in a field with a guitar in her hand and the sea in the background. It wasn't her old guitar. This one was blue, the same blue as the shard of sea beyond the yellow grass. The same blue as her eyes. She looked worn down. There was a handwritten song list. He stared at Birdie, not understanding.

"A friend of hers produced it," she said. As if that explained anything.

"This is great," he said, wanting it to be so and knowing it wasn't. "Why didn't you show it to me before?"

Birdie pressed her lips tightly together. Dec clutched the CD in both hands and stared at it, willing his mother to speak to him. Then Birdie handed him something else, a cream-colored envelope. "This came in March," she said.

He didn't want to take it. He had a powerful sense that there was nothing in it he wanted to hear. She prodded his arm with it until, finally, he snatched it from her. He held it for a long moment before opening it.

It was handwritten but it wasn't Lindy's hand—someone named Anna. He held the letter near the light and started to read. He didn't get far.

Lindy was dead.

There were other words on the cream-colored page but that was the only one he took in. Dead. But then he had already half guessed that from the strange look in Birdie's eyes.

"Lindy sent the CD to *me*," said Birdie. "Not to Bernard, or to you kids. She sent it to the salon. I don't even know how she knew about the salon. But she did."

Dec tried to give her back the letter. She wouldn't take it. He put it on the desk. Then he got to his feet in case she tried to take back the CD. Wasn't that what she was telling him—that it was hers? That she had something over him, over all of them?

"This Anna—she was the one who produced the album. They were friends, I guess. She must have gotten the salon address from Denny. They kept in touch—Denny and Lindy. I guess we all know that now."

Dec was only half listening. Who cared? What difference did it make? Lindy had cut an album and died all in a couple of minutes. He stared at the cover. A moment ago it had seemed like a gift. Now it was a casket. A tiny transparent casket.

"Why didn't you tell me?"

"Because I didn't tell anyone. Not about the CD, not about her dying." Birdie took in a deep breath and then gave it back to the still room. "And not about the other letter, either."

Again she reached into the pocket of the cardigan, and Dec wondered how deep those pockets were, how many more sorrows she was going to dig up.

This letter was on the same stationery, but the writing was Lindy's, and the envelope was addressed to Bernard Steeple. Dec peered at Birdie in disbelief.

"What can I say?" she said. "The damn thing arrived on a Monday. About a year ago. A Monday. The one day of the week I'm home. By sheer luck—if you can call it that—I was the one who went out to get the mail that day. I knew who it was right away, soon as I saw the handwriting. Maybe I'd always expected it. Anyway, I told myself it was fate that I should be the one who found it first." She looked down. "Read it," she said, as if tired of making any more excuses.

The letter was dated August 3, 2002. "Dear Bernard," it started. "I hope you're sitting down!" Dec couldn't read any more. "Just tell me," he said wearily, folding the letter back up and shoving it in the envelope.

"She was looking for money," said Birdie. "She had a chance to make this CD and so she was hitting up Bernard. I was so mad, I didn't know what to do. She said she'd been sick, in the hospital a couple times, but she was doing okay and this project was her one big chance to grab on to her dream."

"So it wasn't just about money."

"She didn't spell it out, Dec. I didn't know how sick. All I knew was that here she was again, out of the blue, looking for something."

Dec stared at Birdie. "She was your best friend."

"Don't remind me."

"Was she asking for a million dollars?"

"No. And it wasn't the money anyway. Bernard's money is his business. I didn't tell him because I was afraid. Afraid that if he got that letter, he'd go to her."

"You don't know that."

"I *did* know it, inside," she said, poking herself in the chest. "And what I learned tonight only proves I was right."

"It doesn't prove anything," said Dec, shaking his head sadly. "You didn't trust him."

She squinted at him through eyes swollen half shut with crying. "Look who's talking about trust," she said. Dec looked away.

"Oh, don't listen to me, Dec," she said. "It's Lindy. Trust gets kind of tied up in a knot where she's concerned. I'd trust your dad to the end of the world, except when it comes to her. Anyway, when the letter arrived, last August, I told myself, if she doesn't hear from him, she'll try again. But she didn't. Then when the CD arrived, I figured, well, that's that. She found the money someplace else. Great. I didn't feel so guilty. I told myself I'd saved Bernard a lot of heartache." She looked straight at Dec. "You read that letter from Anna and try to imagine how guilty I felt when I learned the truth."

They sat, the two of them, in the glow of the little lamp on the desk. An antique flying saucer. The future as it was imagined in the past. Some minutes ticked away. The night moved a little further along the path toward day.

"Did you tell him tonight?"

She shook her head.

"So why are you telling me?"

"I needed to talk to someone," she said. "Whatever the

consequences. I couldn't go on feeling like this. Jealousy is an evil, evil thing. There's no excuse for what I did. But, if you can believe it, I was thinking about your father, too. And you and Sunny."

"That was kind of you." He couldn't keep the sarcasm out of his voice.

She smiled wryly. "I watched you cry your little heart out after Lindy took off. You probably don't remember. I tried to comfort you. I tried to comfort Bernard. About the only one I made any progress with was Sunny. Then, bit by bit, you accepted that I was here to stay and we figured out how to get along. We *have* gotten along, Dec. And, bit by bit, your dad came around, too. I couldn't bear the thought of Lindy getting her claws in him again."

Birdie sighed. She put her hands on her knees and laboriously climbed to her feet. Whatever guilt she might have unburdened, she was weighed down with still more.

"So what am I supposed to do?"

She shook her head. "Whatever you want."

"Is this supposed to be our little secret? Because I'm sick of secrets."

"Tell me about it."

"So?"

She held her hands out at her sides. "I honestly don't know. Tell your dad if you like. I don't care." She headed toward the door. She stopped and leaned against the doorjamb. Then she turned to look at him. "You're a good kid, Dec. I know I let you down. All I can say is I'm sorry."

Dec was too worn-out to speak. She left, and after a moment he followed her to the door. From the railing he saw her shadowy figure cross the entrance hallway and leave the big house. He listened to her car drive off, listened until it was out of earshot. And he wondered just how far she would go.

WHAT I CAN

There was another picture of Lindy inside the liner notes. She was sitting, leaning against a tree in her suede jacket with the eight-inch cowgirl fringe. There was a cigarette between her lips and she was writing something. Under the picture was a little poem and the playlist:

> *This is how I got here, this is who I am.*
> *Don't always do what's smart or good,*
> *Just do the best I can.*

He read the playlist.

Killing Me with Kindness	*Troubled Me*
No Room to Grow	*Out of Eden*
Wildcat Love	*The Way of Stone and Sorrow*
The Boy I Left Behind	*Anna*
Sunshine	*The Water Is Wide*

He couldn't see her face in the picture—it was lost in smoke. It was the jacket he found himself thinking about. He remembered playing with the fringe of it. He remembered how soft it felt. He remembered tracing the Indian embroidery with his finger.

He lay down now in his big red shoe of a childhood bed, with the map-of-the-world comforter pulled over him and his head resting against her picture.

WATCH

He found a stepladder in the basement. He climbed up to the bust of Plato, and carefully—oh, so carefully—laid the statuette on its side. He reached into the cold emptiness of Plato's neck, up into the cavity of his bronze head. There was a little pocket there, made, as far as he could tell, out of paper and glue. There was nothing in the pocket. He hadn't expected there to be.

When Dec went down to Camelot, the Beetle sat in its customary spot in the driveway and Birdie was asleep on a couch in the living room. Sunny was stretched sideways right across the master bed, and his father was scrunched up in Sunny's frilly four-poster, presumably driven there by hard little feet. It was as if the storm of the night before had swept the whole family up and distributed them higgledy-piggledy all over the place. But no one had traveled farther than Dec.

Dec made himself breakfast. The sun poured in like

honey on his toast and made his orange juice glow like something with a current running through it. He made a big pot of coffee. He didn't drink coffee but he had a feeling others might need it.

He couldn't explain it but he felt good. He had found his mother last night. Found her and lost her all in a matter of minutes. Then he had slept deeply and dreamlessly, or so he thought. But leaning against the counter looking out at the crisp yellowness and lush greenness and electric blueness of early June, he wondered if maybe he had been dreaming after all. For he had the strangest feeling that Lindy had come to him, all played out and not angry anymore, and tucked him in one last time. He felt somehow that he had her permission to let her go. After all, she had died a long time ago, really. He had grieved her passing when he was still living in the room with his name on the door. He had built her a boat to carry two when she was not there to sail it any longer. He had missed her and gotten over it.

The smell of coffee wafted through the house and Birdie stirred from her nest of blankets in the living room. He heard her swear. He heard her fingernails clicking as she scrabbled on the coffee table for something. Her cell phone. He heard her talking to Kerrie, asking if she would open up the salon. By the time she had punched the off button, Dec was standing in the living room entranceway with a cup of coffee.

"I figured you might need this," he said.

She seemed almost shy, pulling a blanket across her as if he had never seen her in her old cotton nightie.

"Thank you," she said, avoiding his eyes. A stiff wing of her hair sticking out at a weird angle distracted her and she cursed again. She grabbed a fistful of it. "This is going to require major surgery," she said. He was glad to hear her sound like the Birdie he knew. Chewbacca with bed head. Maybe last night had just been a bad dream. Or maybe he had traveled even farther than he thought. She hefted herself up off the couch. She took the coffee from Dec with a grateful nod.

"Life goes on," he said.

She drove him to school. She placed a freshly picked spray of lilac in the little vase on the dashboard of the Beetle. She had new country on the stereo. Someone was singing about what you have to do to fix a broken heart.

"You were asking your dad about a missing yearbook," she said when they were on the road. "I took it. I was showing Sunny some pictures of her mom and I happened to glance at the stuff kids had written on the autograph pages. There was something of Denny's I didn't want Sunny to see."

Dec understood. One more little mystery cleared up. And now it was his turn.

"I think I know what happened to Dad's watch," he said.

Birdie glanced sideways at him with a puzzled look on her face.

"His father's watch, I mean. The one he wore on D-Day."

"I know *what* you're talking about, Dec. I just have no idea why—of all the things you might have on your mind this morning—you're thinking about an old watch."

Dec wasn't sure he could explain why the watch was important. He only knew that it was, somehow. It explained things that he had no other way of understanding. Who his mother was, who his father was.

"I think Lindy stole that watch and hid it inside Plato's head," he said. "There's a little pocket there, I found it this morning. I think that's what Denny was after when he fell. She must have told him it was really valuable, or something."

Birdie still looked a little anxious. "You've lost me."

"It was her idea of a joke," he said. "She liked to play jokes on Dad. He probably told her that his father's old watch was the most precious thing he owned. I can see him saying that. And so one day when she was really mad at him, she hid it—hid it where he'd never find it." He paused, swallowed. "Just to hurt him."

There, it was out. Dec rolled down the window and took a deep breath of country air. He rolled the window back up.

"How do you know all that?"

"I don't. And no one will ever know. It's totally a guess."

Birdie shook her head a few times. "I've got half a mind to phone up Clare Mahood and tell him your story. You know what that dipstick had the nerve to say at the inquest? He accused your father of killing Runyon in a jealous rage and making it look like an accident. Can you believe anything so nuts?"

"Boy," said Dec. "Go figure."

"I know," said Birdie, laughing. "Talk about ridiculous."

Silence descended on them, leaving them both lost in their own private thoughts. Dec's thinking was particularly tangled. Plato had turned out to be the key to everything. But not in the way Dec had suspected—or feared. He wished Sunny had never put the idea in his mind that Plato might have been on the hall table instead of in its usual spot. She had been wrong and had helped to set him down a treacherous path. He didn't want to think about it. Didn't want to talk anymore, except that there was one thing he needed to say. One thing he needed to get out right away before he had any second thoughts, even though they were pulling up in front of the school.

"It would probably be a good idea if you told Dad about Lindy," he said.

She pulled over to the curb and turned off the radio. "Honesty is always the best policy," she said. But she said it the way a person might say having a molar pulled out with pliers is a good idea.

"Well, it'd save a lot of hassle, don't you think?"

She frowned. She had her perfect pencil-thin eyebrows on again, and she raised one of them expressively. "You think?"

"Yes," said Dec decisively, looking straight ahead. "Then Dad won't have to worry about getting an annulment."

A POEM FOR DEAGLAN

There was a letter for Dec in the post office box. For Deaglan, actually, which was the Irish spelling of his name. Vivien was full of surprises.

in this silence-challenged cafeteria
you sit alone in a room of your own.
are there pictures on the walls in there?
is that what you are frowning at
or why you smile, sometimes, a faraway smile?

i want to knock on your door and say, mister
    look at this
the sun is shining golden on that girl's barrettes
that man is painting his house apricot
the little boy in the sage-green sweater has a brand-new
    trike
the world has ended—i know, i know, i know
    but hey—there's another one!

PICK-UP STICKS

There are tidal pools and great green strands of kelp and drift-wood dry as bone. So much driftwood, like giant pick-up sticks. His dreaming eye focuses in on the driftwood; it begins to tremble. An earthquake, he thinks, but then the logs start to drift up into the air, as if someone has filmed a truckload of logs being dumped off the cliff and then reversed the film. He watches the logs dancing, and then realizes that he is their choreographer. In no time he has himself the skeleton of a wild and wonderful house suspended above the sea. He looks it over from every side with a dream-builder's eye, sees how it might work, how it fits together. He snaps off a whole roll of dream photos, which develop in the darkroom of sleep.

Dec scanned the cliff in the magazine and copied it. He wondered how far it was from where his mother had lived. His mother had talked about California all the time. It was one of her dreams. He had forgotten that, but then she had so many dreams. He had forgotten a lot, but it wasn't a careless kind of forgetting. When she left, he had gathered together everything of hers he could and shoved it down hard into a secret box, locked it and thrown away the key. And then he had found the key and opened up the box. There was more in there than he had bargained for.

Sunny knocked on his bedroom door.

"It's not locked."

She came in wearing powder-blue shorts and a white T-shirt stained pink with Popsicle juice. He showed her his drawings and explained how they worked. There were thin wooden poles and steel cables and floors suspended between them open on every side to the air.

She listened intently and scoured the drawings but with ever-growing perplexity. Her hair was in braids and Dec could see the hearing aid in her right ear. The earaches had stopped, which was great, but he would miss the way she talked as if half her words were capitalized. It had made everything she said seem so urgent.

"It's a funny house," she said, shaking her head.

"It's a pick-up-sticks house."

Sunny laughed. "You're crazy."

Dec smiled and nodded. It *was* kind of crazy. He might have to build a model to show how it worked. He could borrow some of his father's tools, but he would do the work up at his grandfather's workshop in the basement of the big house. He would do this on his own, in his own way. That was the shape of the future.

"Are you going to live in that stick house?" Sunny asked.

"Maybe," he said.

"Will you build me a house, Deckly?" she asked.

"You bet. What kind of a house do you want?"

She thought and thought, then she smiled a very rascally smile. "I want a house that tastes like watermelon juice," she said, and burst out laughing.

LEGS

Dec sat with Ezra on the lawn outside the school. "Ran is totaled," said Ezra. "You owe me three dollars and twenty-seven cents, which is what the insurance guy says it's worth."

"I'll buy you lunch," said Dec.

"Deal," said Ezra. But neither of them moved. It was too beautiful to imagine going indoors. Ezra had decided to write his exams without studying at all, for the fun of it. Dec had just aced history.

"How are things at Camelot?" said Ezra.

Dec shrugged. "Pretty wild," he said. "Birdie's planting an awful lot of petunias and Dad's started to gear up for the Battle of Gettysburg."

"The twentieth-century thing didn't take?"

Dec shook his head. "Too close for comfort, I guess."

He was just about to ask Ezra more about the apartment he had found that weekend in Montreal, when he noticed Vivien across the quad. Ezra saw her, too.

"Hey, Viv," he called.

She waved and started walking toward them but was intercepted en route by the inseparable Melody Fong and Martin McNair. They looked pretty excited about something.

"Probably just proved mathematically why sunshine makes your socks fall down," said Ezra.

"Does it?" asked Dec.

"Well, Martin's socks anyway."

Dec glanced at Martin's socks. But as interesting as they were, his eyes wandered back to Vivien. She wasn't wearing socks. She was wearing pink Birkenstocks and a flowing Indian cotton shift.

"Hey, look," said Dec. "Vivien's got legs!"

She looked his way and waved again. It was one of those I'll-be-there-soon looks, a don't-go-away look.

He nodded. He wasn't going anywhere. Not for the moment. These days, time seemed a roomier place than he ever remembered it.

"Hmmm," said Ezra. "Do I sense some chemistry happening here?"

"Chemistry's my worst subject," said Dec, but he smiled.

Vivien arrived at last and plopped down beside them. "I found this totally cool book at the secondhand store," she said. "The *Esquire Handbook for Hosts.*" She took it from her backpack and opened it. "There's this list at the back, '365 Excuses for a Party.' You want to know what we're celebrating today?"

"I already know," said Dec, smiling. "The world has ended. But hey, there's another one!"